CRUEL CASTLE

BRYONY PEARCE

LOD / T

We hope you enjoy this book.
Please return or renew it by the due date.
You can renew it at **www.norfolk.gov.uk/libraries**
or by using our free library app. Otherwise you can
phone **0344 800 8020** - please have your library
card and pin ready.
You can sign up for email reminders too.

NORFOLK COUNTY COUNCIL
LIBRARY AND INFORMATION SERVICE

NORFOLK ITEM

3 0129 08556 3402

For my readers in the Wirral, who told me how badly
they needed a sequel to *Savage Island* and inspired me
to write it for them.

STRIPES PUBLISHING LIMITED
An imprint of the Little Tiger Group
1 Coda Studios, 189 Munster Road,
London SW6 6AW

www.littletiger.co.uk

Imported into the EEA by Penguin Random House Ireland,
Morrison Chambers, 32 Nassu Street, Dublin D02 YH68

First published in Great Britain in 2021
Text copyright © Bryony Pearce, 2021
Cover castle illustration copyright © Stripes Publishing Limited, 2021
Cover forest illustration copyright © Aleksey Zhuravlev/Shutterstock.com
Floor plan illustrations by Collaborate Agency copyright © Stripes Publishing Limited, 2021
Newspaper image copyright © Picsfive/Shutterstock.com

ISBN: 978-1-78895-321-4

The Forest Stewardship Council® (FSC®) is a global, not-for-profit organization dedicated to the
promotion of responsible forest management worldwide. FSC defines standards based on agreed
principles for responsible forest stewardship that are supported by environmental, social, and economic
stakeholders. To learn more, visit www.fsc.org

10 9 8 7 6 5 4 3 2 1

Who can you trust, when everyone is broken?

They thought Savage Island was the end.
It was only the beginning...

Teens can no longer go for Gold

Billionaire philanthropist, Marcus Gold, has cancelled Iron Teen, the contest that has given teens around the world the chance to win millions. After the plane crash known as the Iron Teen Tragedy which, six months ago, killed all teenaged competitors save one lucky survivor, Grady Jackson, a second disaster has befallen the new batch of contenders, who appear to have ingested a poisonous mushroom during their final meal. The destroying angel, which grows in mixed woodland, contains amatoxin and is so deadly that just a single piece in a soup made from otherwise edible fungi is enough to kill everyone who eats it. It was apparently growing on the island of Aikenhead, although all specimens have now been located and destroyed. Survivor Aanay Bukhari told reporters that he was the only who one who did not eat the

Stowerling Keep: Ground Floor

Key

- Window
- Steps
- Lift
- Fireplace
- Doorway
- Bathroom
- Closet
- Balcony
- Coal chute

Rooms and Areas

Dining Room
Kitchen
Pantry
Laundry
Servants' Quarters
Steps to Cellar
Stairs to First Floor and Basement
Entrance Hall
Armoury
Music Room
Steps to Games Room
Library
Mezzanine
Gallery
Exit to Garden
Kitchen Garden
Lake
Fountains
Lawn
Greenhouses
Orchard
Rose Garden
Forecourt
Lift
Guest Bed 1
Guest Bed 2
Garage / Old Stables

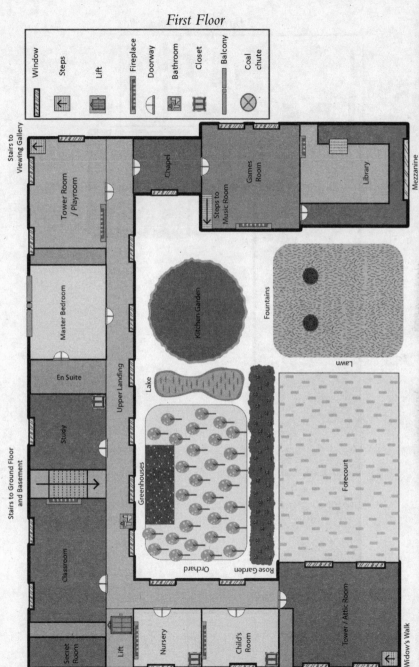

First Floor

Legend:
- Window
- Steps
- Lift
- Fireplace
- Doorway
- Bathroom
- Closet
- Balcony
- Coal chute

Stairs to Viewing Gallery

Stairs to Ground Floor and Basement

Tower Room / Playroom

Master Bedroom

En Suite

Study

Classroom

Secret Room

Lift

Nursery

Child's Room

Upper Landing

Chapel

Kitchen Garden

Lake

Greenhouses

Orchard

Rose Garden

Fountains

Lawn

Forecourt

Games Room

Steps to Music Room

Library

Mezzanine

Tower / Attic Room

Widow's Walk

Steps to Widow's Walk

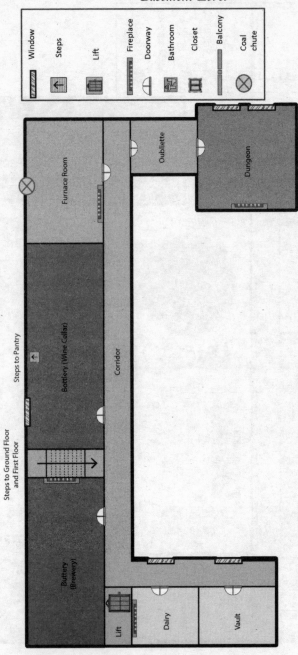

Basement Level

Key:
- Window
- Steps
- Lift
- Fireplace
- Doorway
- Bathroom
- Closet
- Balcony
- Coal chute

Rooms:
- Furnace Room
- Oubliette
- Dungeon
- Bottlery (Wine Cellar)
- Corridor
- Buttery (Brewery)
- Lift
- Dairy
- Vault

Steps to Pantry

Steps to Ground Floor and First Floor

Where It All Finished

Ben

Grady's hands were round my throat and I was too weak
to fight him off. I was going to die but I couldn't bring
myself to care. I turned my face from his and found Lizzie's.
She was lying in the sand where I had left her; one cheek
submerged in the rolling surf almost as if she was watching
me. I'm coming, *I thought.* Wherever you are, wait
for me.

Grady put his mouth next to mine as he squeezed, as
though he wanted to feel my last breath against his. Then he
turned. His lips found my ear and I shuddered, my muscles
twitching, the instinct to survive battling with my desire to
follow the girl I had loved since I was six years old.

"She's not dead."

I jerked, unable to comprehend. His words: whirling,
meaningless syllables. I blinked slowly and realized that
while Grady was still shaking me, he wasn't squeezing as
tightly. I could breathe.

"She's not dead." The words came again. "Remember

my medical kit? I slipped her a bunch of sleeping pills." I twisted, trying to look him in the eye, but his face remained too close. "I'm serious," he hissed. "She's taken an overdose – her heart rate and respiration are way down. It's enough to fool Gold's cameras but she should wake up tomorrow." Grady swallowed, so close that I could feel the lurch of his Adam's apple. "What I did to Carmen… Someone was going to die, and she was already so badly hurt. It made sense for it to be her. But I won't be made to perform like a monkey. I've got more pills. If you reach for my shirt pocket, you'll find them."

I stared at Lizzie with Grady's hands still pressed against my throat. Was it possible? Was her pallor just sea-cold and not death, as I'd assumed. I was no doctor. I didn't really know how to tell. Or was Grady toying with me? An additional cruelty before he killed me. Gold had said he was a psychopath, like my brother. Maybe he needed a little more spice with his murder. Hope before a final twist of the knife.

"I can't drag this out much longer," Grady whispered. "The cameras are on us – they're everywhere. This won't seem real if you don't hurry."

I groped for his chest with stiff fingers and found his pocket. With my hand between our bodies, it would appear *as if I was trying to shove him off me. I pushed my fingers inside and felt pills. I scraped them into my palm. I had no idea how many: more than three, less than ten. I pulled my hand free and put it to my mouth, then I hesitated.*

"Trust me," Grady hissed.

I didn't. He'd sided with Gold and killed Carmen. But ... what choice did I have? Either I took this chance or he strangled me. What difference did it make? I looked at Lizzie's face and pressed my palm against my lips. The pills tumbled on to my tongue and into my throat, choking me.

"Drum your heels against the ground," Grady instructed. "It'll look as if you're dying."

I am dying, I thought. My head started to spin and even though I was lying on the cold grit of the beach, I felt as if I was going to fall off. My limbs grew heavy and I gripped Grady as terror momentarily gave me strength. I felt sick, but nothing came up. Instead I went down.

Down.

Down.

▼

I kick the covers off as I wake with a scream. It's the same every night, that memory of dying. I roll over and off the bed, holding my head in my shaking hands, my eyes raw and aching. I know I won't see Lizzie when I open them. The nightmares are worse when she leaves the room as if I know, even when unconscious, that she has abandoned me to them.

Knowing there will be no more sleep, I stagger into the dingy bathroom of the Welsh bed and breakfast (cash payments, no questions asked) and stare into the mirror.

Will stares back at me. It's crazy how much I look like him now, with my ginger hair dyed brown and grown out.

I touch the cold glass. "Well, I slept on it." I run my finger down the curve of his – my – cheek. I twist my mouth into his sardonic smile. "I said I would, and I did. So, what do you think, Will?" I lean closer, putting my forehead against his. "Should we help Grady?"

Chapter One

Grady

"A stranger is a friend you haven't met yet." That's what my mother used to say. Of course, that was before my father did a number on her and she killed herself.

Anyway, she was wrong. Not just about my father, otherwise she would never have married the good doctor, but about *everything*. A stranger isn't *a friend I haven't met yet*. A stranger is *a puzzle I haven't solved yet*.

That's what I see when I look at you. Your face is one of those sliding puzzles – move the pieces in the right configuration and I get the picture I want: a smile, a laugh, tears, anger … rage. You are nothing more than a puzzle. A simple one. What makes you work? What will make you offer to carry my bag, protect me from danger or push you over the edge? What will turn you into my ace in the hole, waiting to take on Gold for me, if I need you to?

I'm not *broken*, my father was clear about that. No, I'm *better* than you. If you weren't so easy to solve, I wouldn't be able to get you to do what I want. It's your own fault.

Click, shush, click, shush. I don't need to look up to know that Bella just shimmied into the break room, her short skirt brushing toned, tanned skin, her high heels tapping against tile. I don't need to look up, but I do. I can appreciate art, although I've always been more of a Cubist person. I'm sure that Picasso saw people the same way as I do. In pieces.

She's striking a pose against the door frame. Even the smallest gesture of hers is calculated according to its aesthetic. She won't move until I show some appreciation. Today her lustrous black hair is curling down her back, pinned at the front to pull it away from her high cheekbones and cat-like black eyes.

Knowing it's what she needs, I give her a smile and let appreciation shine in my eyes. With a purr of satisfaction, she sashays into the room.

"Grady." Her voice is mellow and smooth. She has an Italian accent and in her mouth the *ay* in my name is emphasized, the *ee* sound falling away. "Aren't you meant to be working, *caro*?" She carefully shifts a few degrees, so her ass is facing me, bends down to open the fridge and removes a mineral water. She turns her head to look at me over her shoulder. "Those charts won't analyze themselves."

I allow a hitch into my breath as I reply. "I've run all the numbers. Just taking a break before I write up my findings."

"You're almost done?" She twists off the top then tips her head back to drink, allowing me to watch the bobbing column of her throat.

"Y-yes." The stutter is deliberate. She smiles around the bottle.

"So, perhaps, Grady, you could take a look at mine? You're so much faster than I am." She touches a finger to her mouth, wiping a bead of water away with her fingertip.

I wonder for a moment how hard I should make her work for it. She has given me a show and it would be no skin off my nose. Numbers are easy, if boring. Let her think she has me, that I'm curled round her little finger. It'll be all the more effective when I take it back.

"Sure, Bella." I let myself sound pathetic. I know what she sees when she looks at me — an amusing conspiracy theorist carrying a layer of fat round my waist that no amount of exercise can shift, a rumpled suit, glasses that I've recently adopted. "Did you know that the CIA operates an illegal drug cartel?" I add enthusiastically.

Bella laughs. "Meet me at my desk and I'll show you the work you can help with, Grady."

I'm harmless. I'm the guy next door. I'm the one no one would ever believe could hurt them.

And yet...

As Bella glides out, she glances back, her expression momentarily speculative. This place looks like an office, but it isn't. It's a shark tank. And Bella has to be wondering, am I really that much of a minnow?

"You shouldn't let her do that to you." Aanay had been standing behind the cupboard the whole time. Bella hadn't even noticed him. He spends as much time in here as he can, away from the rest of the predators.

I arrange my mouth into the shape of a smile. "I don't mind."

"I shouldn't care, but..." He blushes. "You're better than that."

I shrug, push my empty coffee mug to one side,

and stand. "If I don't do her work, she might lose her place on the programme and then what would we have to look at?"

"You really think she'd lose her place on the programme?" Aanay looks up, hope shining in his eyes. I don't think it had occurred to him that he could get himself kicked off the grad scheme by being a poor employee. It's all I've been thinking about. I just haven't worked out the best way of failing, without the kind of retribution that would surely follow.

"Honestly?" I sigh. "No, I don't. Gold wants the work done, so does it matter how it happens? She's effective at getting her quotas met. This isn't about how good we are at the job – it's about showing we can run a company. The people who work for Bella Russo will be *very happy and extremely productive.*"

Aanay blushes again, the colour creeping up his collar and over his cheeks. I fight the instinct to apologise. He's so quiet, so still, sometimes I want to do something to make him yell swear words.

He doesn't want to be here any more than I do. I tilt my head and watch his flush deepen. How did he even *get* on to Gold's graduate programme?

I can't see him doing what I did. I can't see him committing murder. But … maybe *he's* a great white shark in disguise as a minnow. Maybe he's the best actor in here.

One day I'll find out.

He holds out his hand for my empty cup and when I give it to him, he starts to wash it up.

"You cleaning for us now, Bukhari?" The clones move in a school and now they're here, all six of them: Aamon, Bram, Damien, Jason, Dawson and Bates. They're the same as far as I can tell. All white males, all dressed in matching two-piece suits, all dead-eyed.

Before I'd been forced to work in Gold's London office, there'd been the island. We'd thought it would be three days of fun with a huge cash prize at the end. We hadn't known it was Gold's recruitment ground; that he was looking for psychopaths to employ in his corporation. He wanted ruthless business leaders to take over his various companies, and he wanted videos of them doing terrible things, so they would never go against his orders. We hadn't realized that the cash prize would come with a price: a job offer, and that turning it down was not an option.

I won the game on the island. I earned the cash prize, the job offer … and a lifetime of servitude under Marcus Gold.

I'd say I sold my soul, but I don't believe I ever had one.

There'd been another boy on Aikenhead, Reece Armstrong. He'd been the one to start the violence: he cut off Carmen's hand. He'd have fitted in very well with the clones.

Carmen killed him in the end. And I killed Carmen. I look at my hands. The brutality of it all came as a bit of a shock, but in the end it wasn't so bad. Still, after killing Carmen I decided it would be the last time. If killing needs to be done, I'll manipulate others into doing it for me.

When Gold insisted that I exterminate Lizzie and Ben, I decided not to. Why should I bow to anyone?

I let Lizzie live in order to keep Ben onside, and I kept Ben alive in case I needed a trump card. We were lucky that Gold wanted only his own people to see the bodies. He offered to pay for the funerals of all those killed on the island, as long as they were cremated right away. Ben and Lizzie woke in the morgue, swapped their toe tags with corpses, and ran. I don't know or care whose ashes their families cry over.

▼

"You're a great little servant, Bukhari," Jason drawls. "Let's hear you say, 'what can I do for you today, sir?'"

I wonder for a moment whether to get involved or stand back. There are six of them and one of me. I can't say there are two of us because Aanay won't stand up for himself. Soon I'll find out why he's so determined to be such a doormat.

Ben wouldn't have hesitated; he'd have already been yelling at Jason. Lizzie would have simply launched herself at Dawson, and Will would have joined in, just because he loved to hurt people. If Ben had been here, no one would have dared touch Aanay.

I'm not Ben.

I know how this will play out. They'll humiliate Aanay, he'll take it. They probably won't hurt him. I can walk away.

But … they think Aanay is my friend. If I walk away, they'll see me as weak. This is a shark tank. The weak get eaten.

On the *other* hand, I don't get my hands dirty. "Hey!" I call. "Bella, can you step in here a minute?"

The boys had been moving to surround Aanay and myself, but now they freeze.

"You—" Bram starts.

Click, swish, click, swish.

Bella steps into the room and assesses the situation. "*Buongiorno*, boys. What is the problem, Grady?" An eyebrow rises.

"Just wanted to let you know it might be a little while before I can get to your spreadsheets." I allow a little tremble into my voice, a slight stutter.

Bella's eyes narrow. "That won't do, Grady." She looks at Dawson. He's watching her, his fingers tapping almost unconsciously against the notebook he keeps in his trouser pocket. I make a mental note to get a look inside that thing.

"We're just havin' a bit of fun, Bella," he says, his cockney accent the one thing that makes him stand out among the clones. "It's our break, innit?"

"Grady's break is over." Bella steps forwards and

13

touches a finger to the button of Dawson's navy suit jacket. She plays with it gently, then gives it a sudden twist. "He's already agreed to help me."

"*Grady* can go," Jason snaps, his eyes tight on Aanay.

Bella looks at me and I shrug, as if helpless. She sighs. "*And* Aanay. I'm certain that he has work of his own to be doing." She leans in as if to whisper in Dawson's ear. "Christopher Gold is coming to inspect the floor. I think we should *all* have work to show him, don't you?"

Dawson swallows. "Gold's son?"

Bella steps back from him. "He texted me." She holds up her phone with a slight smile.

"Why would he…" Jason leans to snatch the phone from her, but Dawson slaps his hand away.

"Don't touch her."

Jason curls a lip, shakes his hand and leans back again.

"You *know* why he would text me." Bella's smile is sultry.

Dawson's eyes flick to her lips, then back to her eyes. His own are cloudy with disappointment. "Yes, Bella."

She straightens his tie and speaks to me without looking away from Dawson. "Grady, go!"

Jason and Bates watch with narrowed eyes as I reach back, grab Aanay and scuttle from the room, dragging him with me. At least now they know I'll put up a fight, in my own way. They'll be looking for payback, but what's new?

This office is filled with psychopaths. I can't be any more alert to danger than I already am.

Chapter Two

Lizzie

Ben is talking to himself again. He thinks I haven't noticed but he's staring into the mirror and his mutters are like rats crawling up the inside of the walls of this creepy B&B.

It's something he's been doing since leaving the island. He has always been, quite literally, his brother's keeper and I honestly think Will's death has broken him. One moment he'll be Ben, the next his eyes are dead and he's gone. He never remembers.

I rub the heel of my hand against my temple. This headache is worse than usual; it's the stress. I stare at my burner phone, wishing desperately that I could call home and find out how Dad's doing. He thinks I'm dead, killed in the plane crash Gold faked. If I call home and let him know I'm OK, Gold will find out. He'll track us down and this time there'll be no escape.

According to my aunt's Facebook, the cancer

is killing Dad. I want more than anything to be there for him, but I can't. This whole situation is my fault. *I* found the Iron Teen contest, *I* talked Ben and Carmen into going. It's my fault Carmen's dead. I'm to blame for Will's death. Ben has fragmented because of me. If it was just me, I'd risk it and call home. But I can't put Ben in danger. Anyway, I deserve this pain.

I need to think. We're talking to Matt from Corruption Watch again later. It's an NGO – I found it online and made some calls. They're usually more interested in the arms trade than corporations like Gold's, but Matt saw right away that Gold's long-term plan for a kind of capitalist global domination can't be allowed to succeed. Not to mention all the teenagers left dead in his wake.

I'm not completely sure he believes us, and he can't do a thing without proof (our being alive isn't enough to take down Gold), but at least he's interested in our story.

I could go and put my arms round Ben, talk to him.

He once said he loved me. But what would I say to him now? "Sorry, your brother's dead because I wanted an adventure."

I drag my nails through my hair. Even that feels wrong. It's been short since I lopped off my plaits with nail scissors when I was twelve. Now I've grown it and bleached it from raven-black to a dirty blond. It reaches my shoulders and is as dry as straw thanks to the peroxide. It may be a disguise, but I hate it.

I've also had to give up the glasses I loved. I have a choice between thick-rimmed NHS specials or contact lenses, because neither look like *me*. Mostly I wear the contacts. My eyes are bloodshot and bleary thanks to the constant headaches.

"I'm sorry, Ben," I whisper. "I'm sorry I broke you." My eyes go to the Gold International uniforms hanging on the back of the bathroom door. Grady took them from a cleaner weeks ago and sent them to our PO box. They dangle there, part of a plan that hasn't come together yet, a promise that one day soon we'll take down Gold.

Gold is a billionaire with the resources of a small country. We have two cleaning uniforms, a couple of miniature cameras from a Christmas catalogue and the somewhat sceptical ear of an assistant at an

NGO. Somehow, we have to make it work.

We just need something else to fall into place and then we'll have a chance to go home. We're just waiting for Grady.

Chapter Three

Grady

Bella was right, Christopher Gold is here. She hadn't been lying to save my hide, and now he's stalking the floor like Donald Trump in the White House, glancing at computer screens, flicking through reports and occasionally leaning down to comment in the ear of a smirking clone. When he speaks to Dawson, Dawson stiffens, as if he doesn't like what Gold is saying. Then Gold claps him on the back and crooks a finger at Bella.

She goes to him, smiling, touching his arm. He speaks low in her ear and I watch her go from preening to pale. Then he walks on and leaves her standing there.

In my opinion, Gold has embraced his name a little strongly. His hair is golden blond, swept back from his face, an expensive cut. His glasses are gilt-rimmed, he sports a golden tan and his tie shimmers with the gold thread running through it. He looks like his father, or like his father would have looked twenty years ago: the same wide jaw, narrow nose and close-set, dead eyes.

As he draws nearer to our little corner of the office, Aanay starts to shake. He's been staring at his screensaver since Gold arrived, literally terrified out of his mind. Frankly he's starting to make even me feel nervous.

"Can't you stop that?" I whisper. "You're freaking me out."

There's one other person Gold has yet to speak to: Iris Pyrite. It looks as if he's detouring via her desk on his way to see us. She sits on her own, under the long window that overlooks the London skyline. It's the best seat in the house but I've never seen her appreciate the view. She sits, as always, with her ankles crossed, her skirt pulled down to her knees, silk blouse buttoned to her throat. Her suit jacket folded carefully over the back of her chair. Her hair, like Gold's, is blond, a dark, almost coppery shade, and her eyes are ice-blue. Her skin is pale, not a single freckle, and her nose is what they used to call aquiline. Bella looks as if she's on track to make or marry money. Iris looks as if she comes from money.

She's barely said two words to me in the four months I've been here. In fact, I've never seen her have a conversation with anyone. She never takes a lunch break, only drinks water. I'd love to know what she did to get on the grad programme. I wonder if she got those pale fingers dirty.

Gold speaks to her in a low tone. Her facial expression remains unchanged, but I'm watching closely and I see her fingers grip the desk and tighten until her nails redden.

I glance at Aanay. "What do you think he's saying to her?" Aanay ignores me. His eyes are tightly closed. I lower my own gaze as Gold saunters in my direction. He stops behind me and I turn my screen, making sure he can see the results of the project I'm working on.

"Grady Jackson." He pitches his voice so that only Aanay and I can hear him. I nod without turning to face him. His hand comes down on my shoulder, pressing hard; the signet ring with the Gold International logo on it glitters in my periphery. "You've been a bad boy." His voice is hoarfrost. Anyone else saying that would have done so with a smirk, Gold is simply stating a fact, like 'The queen is a lizard person'.

My mind races. I've been a *bad boy*. There's only one thing this could be: Gold has discovered that Ben and Lizzie are alive. Perhaps I hadn't covered the money trail as well as I'd thought. Or maybe they've found one of my burner phones. Or was I recorded stealing the uniforms after all?

I lick my lips delicately. "I don't know what you—"

"Shut it, Jackson." He speaks mildly. I haven't annoyed him; my denial is nothing more than he expects. "Be in the boardroom in five minutes. Any attempt to leave the building will be viewed ... dimly." He squeezes my shoulder in gentle warning.

I raise my eyes and see Aanay staring at me, his lips frozen in panic. Neither of us move or speak. Gold walks from my side of the desk to Aanay's.

"You're a Jain, is that right, Bukhari?"

Aanay nods, relieved to be asked such an easy question.

"So, you never lie."

Aanay shakes his head so hard his fringe flaps like raven wings, as if trying to lift him out of his seat. Gold pulls a piece of paper from his pocket and consults it briefly. "You don't lie, you won't commit violence, you don't care about material goods, you don't steal –" he hesitates – "you live a 'chaste life'. That's what you told my father and our surveillance of you bears that out ... so far."

Aanay nods again, his cheeks are bloodless. Is he going to faint?

"You can join Jackson in the boardroom. It'll be interesting to see how you react to his lies."

Aanay sways.

"Breathe, Aanay," I murmur. Gold is walking away. Aanay looks as if he's going to bolt. "You can't run, remember what he said. It'll be viewed ... dimly."

"Oh, Grady!" Aanay exhales. "What have you done? ... And what are you going to do?"

The boardroom is at the other end of the office. To reach it I will have to propel Aanay past Iris, Bella and the clones. I have less than five minutes.

"I need to go to the bathroom." My voice is hoarser than I intend it to be.

Aanay just looks at me; I think he's in shock.

24

"I'm coming back, Aanay." I lower my voice. "Don't go *anywhere* without me."

He doesn't react, just closes his eyes. I get to my feet and walk carefully towards the bathrooms. I can't run, just going to the toilet, nothing to see here. I spot Dawson rising and put on a burst of speed. I don't have time to speak to anyone. I have *five* minutes, maybe four now.

I skid past the lift and into the men's room and realize that, despite my efforts, I *have* broken into a run. I slam the door and hurl myself into the nearest cubicle. I have about three minutes. My bladder burns. No time to pee.

As quietly as I can, I lift the back off the toilet. Ceramic scrapes noisily and I wince. For a moment my eyes blur and I'm sure that it's gone, but then they clear and the bag wavers into view. It's taped to the inside of the cistern – a white bag against white ceramic, under water. You'd have to know it was there to find it. I inhale shakily, reach in and pull the bag out. The burner phone is dry but taking forever to switch on. I stare at it, praying it hasn't died on me.

Finally, the screen brightens.

I type in the number from memory. My fingers fumble against the keys. I enter the wrong digits, delete them and start again. My heartbeat counts down the seconds. They'll come for me if I take too long.

There's only one message I can send.

Get out

The phone is on silent, but I wait until the 'message sent' icon appears. One minute left. I delete the message, wipe my prints off the phone and toss it back in the bag without switching it off. I drop it back into the cistern and close it up. Then I flush the toilet and head to the sinks where I splash my face and glance up at the camera. Of course there's surveillance in here, but I'm ninety per cent sure that no one is recording in the cubicles.

I have seconds left. I leave the toilet and head back towards my desk to pick up Aanay. There's a security guard standing by the lift now. He wasn't there before. He watches me go.

Chapter Four

Lizzie

I jump when my phone beeps with an incoming message. The noise is vulgar in the muffled quiet. For a moment surprise makes me stupid, but then I glance down.

Get out

I gape for a second and then leap to my feet. "*Ben!*"

He hears the urgency in my voice, but there is still a hesitation before he barrels into the bedroom. For an instant when I see him come in, I almost think it's Will. Who'd have thought that some dye and a haircut would make Ben look so different? At least if I hardly recognize him, then Gold won't either.

I hold the phone out to show him. Ben takes in the message and is at the wardrobe before I can take another step. He drags two holdalls from the bottom and yanks them open. He tosses the Gold

27

International uniforms inside, followed by our stash of money, our fake IDs and the three remaining burner phones from behind the rotten skirting board.

I snap our laptop closed, wrap it in a jumper, snag the miniature cameras I was testing and shove them into the other bag. Then I run into the bathroom and sweep my contacts inside. Everything else we can leave. I run for the door, but Ben catches my arm. "Use the window."

I turn round, pull up the sash and drop my bag carefully through the opening. There is a thud as it hits the ground and I wince, hoping the jumper has protected the laptop. I scramble on to the sill and look down. We're on the first floor. It's a drop, but nothing I can't handle. I'm a climber; I've jumped from higher. I leap, and as I land, tuck and roll on to my shoulder and back to my feet in one smooth movement.

Ben's holdall follows and he comes after it, gasping as his feet hit the ground.

"You forgot to roll!"

"It doesn't matter." He picks up his bag. "Go!"

We're in a walled courtyard behind an alleyway. In front of us there's a broken garden chair. An ashtray sits beside it, filled with cigarette butts swimming in half an inch of dirty rainwater.

I eye the wall. "What if they're waiting for us?"

"We've got to assume they'll go round the front. They won't know we're expecting them."

"But if Grady—"

"We've no choice, Lizzie." His tone is impatient. It's not very … Ben-like. In fact, something in his voice reminds me of his brother. That's been happening more often recently. Maybe with Will in the picture, Ben had no choice but to be the good guy. Now Will is gone, Ben is free. He can be who he wants to be. I supress a shiver. Is it possible that I hadn't known Ben Harper as well as I'd thought?

He drags the chair to the wall and climbs on to it. He's favouring his right leg.

"Your ankle is twisted." I tug him off the chair. "It could be sprained. At least let me go first. I can run if I have to, you can't."

"OK, fine." Ben shifts the holdall so he's wearing it like a rucksack and watches me climb the wall.

The alley below is deserted. "I can't see anyone. I'm going over."

For a moment it looks as if he's going to object,

the over-protective idiot, but then he nods and I flip myself on to the other side, landing lightly on my toes.

He follows, landing with a wince, then he takes my hand.

I look anxiously towards the road. "Where do we go?"

"The library, at least for now. It should be empty and we can hide out till the next bus."

I nod and we step on to the street. The pub will be getting busy with the lunchtime crowd soon, and there's a primary school at the end of the road with a playground that will fill with kids, but other than that it's quiet. It always is here. Apart from the occasional hiker, this isn't a part of Wales that sees tourists, it's just a dead end with mountains in the background and grey skies all year round.

I leave my hand in Ben's as we stride jerkily towards the library. I want to run but running draws more attention, it makes people remember you. I keep my head down, letting my hair fall over my face, wishing I'd thought to throw on my hoodie.

Ben squeezes my fingers. "We'll be OK. We knew this was a possibility."

All I can think is that I might as well have called my dad.

I look at Ben. "What do you think Grady's *done*?"

Chapter Five

Grady

Christopher Gold is already sitting at the head of the long boardroom table. I narrow my eyes. The five minutes I was given were so that he could get into position.

There's a window behind the table. It's big enough for a person to jump through … or be heaved out of. There's a bottle of water and two heavy-based glasses in the centre of the table. There's only one door – one way in and out. Gold is alone but I feel the cameras on me. I look up. There's one in the centre of the ceiling by the light fitting and another in each corner of the room. Every angle covered.

Gold has a folder in front of him. He says nothing, only opens it, takes out two photographs and slides them across to us.

Aanay takes one look, staggers to the corner and begins to retch. I peer at the pictures. One is of Carmen. She's lying on the floor in the control room of the island, where I killed her. She has been rolled to face the photographer and her shirt pushed up to show the bloody wound. I had stabbed her carefully, holding the blade flat and sliding it between the third and fourth ribs, into her liver. It was a quick death, a kindness.

I examine her face. Her eyes are open, staring blankly at the camera, and although her pink-tipped hair has been pushed back from her face, strands are stuck to her bloody lips. Her one remaining hand is curled slightly and covered in drying blood, her stump is thrown outwards, as if to catch the beam of light that slices the floor beside her.

I shift my eyes to the other photo. It's Aanay. Only it isn't. When I look closer, I see a girl who looks like Aanay, except older. She has been stabbed too, but nowhere near as compassionately as Carmen was. This is a messy wound, poorly placed. She must have taken ages to bleed out. Her blood surrounds her in a crimson inkblot of wings, with her body at the centre. Her eyes are closed, her face pinched with pain.

Aanay is crying now. His sobs reverberate through the boardroom. Gold curls his lip in mild disgust.

Using one finger, I slide the pictures back over the table. "Message received."

"Is it?" Gold looks at the photo of Carmen, his head cocked to one side. "My father *thought* the message had already been effectively delivered. We *own* you. And yet…"

I glance at the water. "May I?"

Gold gestures and I pour myself half a glass. If I'm fast, I can smash it on the table and hold a shard to Gold's jugular, walk us out of the building.

I take a careful sip, keeping my eyes on Gold. The security guard can't be far. There'll be a panic button under the table. I need to get Gold to move away from it. Perhaps I'll ask for his help with Aanay, it looks as if he'll need carrying out of here.

"You have nothing to say for yourself?" Gold's eyes narrow.

I adjust my glasses. "The idea of being owned is not a comfortable one for me."

"And so, this rebellion." Gold slides another document out of his folder. Not a document, a magazine. A copy of *The Con,* the first copy I'd had professionally printed with my 'winnings'.

"Bukhari, if you please." Gold hands the magazine

to Aanay, who looks up with tears in his eyes.

"W–what?"

"I'd like you to read out the article marked on page two, please."

"I–I–"

"In your own time." His tone meant *do it now.*

Aanay lurches towards Gold, takes the magazine and glances at me.

The cover has a Google image of an island on it. It isn't Aikenhead, there *are* no pictures of Aikenhead, but it is another Shetland Isle and I'm certain the smudge in the distance *is* the right one. Above the picture is the magazine's title: *The Con: Conspiracies you can believe.* Then *What happens on the secret islands of the mega-rich?*

I'd written it before I was '*invited*' to London to enter the graduate programme, when I'd thought there was still a chance that they'd deliver my winnings and forget about me. When I believed I'd be able to live my own life, uncovering conspiracies from the flat I intended to buy.

Pages rustled as Aanay opened the magazine.

"*There's an island north of mainland Scotland owned by one of the richest men in the world. People die there…*"

Aanay stumbles through the sentence and stares at me. "You didn't?"

I shrug, but my mind is racing. "I don't name names." I adjust my glasses again, as if nervous, but I'm elated. Is *this* all they've discovered – an old copy of *The Con*? They don't know about my theft of the uniforms, that Ben and Lizzie are still alive, or that I've been sending them money. They don't know about the burner phones or the B&B in Wales.

They don't know.

Aanay is stuttering his way through the article, but I'm not listening to him, I'm watching Gold watching me. Eventually he holds up a hand. "Enough."

I hunch my shoulders as if frightened. I make my hands shake as I take my glasses off, polish them and put them back on again.

Gold looks at Aanay. "Has he printed any more of these?"

Aanay blinks. "I–I don't know. I didn't know about this."

"Does he talk about 'conspiracies'?"

Aanay glances at me and then away again. "Yes."

"A lot?"

36

"A-all the time." Aanay shoves his hands into his pockets, his back stiff, his shoulders trembling. "I'm sorry, Grady."

"It's all right, Aanay." I look at Gold. "You knew my ambition. I talked about starting *The Con* when I was on Aikenhead, don't tell me your people weren't listening. You know conspiracies are my … obsession. If someone like Gold has this kind of plan, a global federation of companies run by people like us, all controlled by him, then what else is out there? The puzzle is fascinating. I like to see pieces coming together. Why would I give that up?"

"Because we're telling you to." Gold tosses *The Con* into the empty waste bin in the corner. "We thought it went without saying that you weren't to reveal the truth of what happened on Aikenhead. Everyone else got that message. Why not you?"

"I don't mention any names," I repeat stubbornly.

Gold sits back. "Luckily for you, Jackson, we looked into it. You have all of thirty subscribers to your little 'magazine'." He sneers. "Basement-dwellers, teens into cosplay and forty-year-old men living with their mothers. No flags have been raised, no added scrutiny on Aikenhead or Gold International.

You've got away with it. This time."

"You mean *you* got away with it," Aanay says, surprising me.

"Quite right, Bukhari. We got away with it. As we always do." Gold leans back and rests his hands on the table in front of him. His signet ring catches the light.

"However, we do have a few issues with this batch of recruits and so we are doing something we haven't had to do in quite some time."

Aanay shoots a look at me and I try to send calming vibes in his direction. Gold said I'd got away with it, so it seems right that I should look relieved. I allow my shoulders to relax.

"We're sending you on a team-bonding exercise," Gold finishes.

"Team bonding," I say slowly. "Aanay and myself?"

Gold nods.

"This is going to be like the island, isn't it?" I find myself unable to look at Aanay.

"Not at all." Gold smiles and I clench my fists. "My father owns a castle in Scotland: Stowerling Keep. It's very private, very remote. Perfect for our needs."

"Our needs?"

"Team bonding," he repeats. "Of course, you'll be observed doing your activities."

"Activities like..."

"Team-bonding activities." Gold's smile does not widen, nor does it vanish. "If I tell you any more it'll ruin the surprise, won't it, Jackson?"

I nod. He knows I'm not stupid, he knows that I know I'm being punished. Is he sending Aanay with me as an additional penalty, or has Aanay himself done something to bring down their ire?

Stowerling Keep. It's going to make Aikenhead look like Disneyland.

"When do we—?"

"You have two days, Jackson. Be here on Saturday morning at the usual time. Pack an overnight bag. A car will be waiting." He smiles again. This time it reaches his eyes. "Monday morning you'll be back in the office, bright and early. You may even be in line for a promotion." He lays his hand on the folder containing the photographs of Carmen and Aanay's sister. "You know what will happen if you don't show up, of course."

"Of course."

"Bukhari?"

Aanay gives the slightest nod. "If my parents find out what really happened to Indrani, it will kill them."

"Let's make sure they don't. Saturday morning, Bukhari. You can travel with Jackson." He stands and goes to the window. "It's been a long time since we've opened Stowerling Keep," he says. "I'm very much looking forward to it."

Chapter Six

Ben

The librarian is glaring at us. You'd think she'd be happy about having someone in the building, but Lizzie's incoming text practically shook the dust off the books and she isn't pleased.

I pull Lizzie into the corner marked *Adult Thriller*, making the most of the excuse to touch her. She looks different with her hair blond and her contact lenses in. She's obviously still having those headaches too. She's lost weight and she's less focused than she was, but my heart still beats for her. It always used to be Lizzie in charge, but I have to take the lead more and more often now. It's as if she doesn't trust herself.

"What does it say?" I point at the phone and she holds it up.

Stand down

"False alarm." Lizzie's smile is faint. "That's a relief. I wonder what happened."

"We can go back to the B&B," I say, but Lizzie

shakes her head.

"Not just yet. I'm sick of those four walls."

I nod my understanding. "There's a computer in the corner. The librarian can't see it from her desk. Let's go over there."

Lizzie squeezes my hand gratefully and I lead her to the chair, pulling up another one at her side.

Another message beeps in, followed by a loud *tut* from the other side of the room. I take the phone from Lizzie, switch it to silent and look at Grady's new text.

Stowerling Keep, this weekend. Saturday start.

Lizzie's eyes meet mine. I reach past her and switch on the computer.

"You have to pay for that." The librarian's voice is sharp. I guess she can see us after all. I go to pay her for an hour.

When I get back, Lizzie has moved across so that I have the seat in front of the keyboard.

"What's Stowerling Keep?" she asks, and I type it in.

There're a couple of articles on Google describing it as a castle in Scotland, owned by the Gold family. There's even an address and a photograph. It looks less like a castle than a fortified mansion. There are only two floors but there are turrets, one at either side. The stone glows coppery in the sunlight. There's woodland to one side and what looks like a beach to the other. It's idyllic.

"How come this is online?" Lizzie is staring at the photograph. "It's like Aikenhead doesn't exist, but this is all right here."

"Maybe because it's an old family house. You can't just hide a castle."

"He hid an island."

I shrug. "What do you think is going on there?"

"Grady must think it's something we can use against Gold." Lizzie rubs her head again. "Can we even get there by Saturday morning? And how do we get inside?"

I bring up a train timetable and we examine it. "We can get there late Friday night."

Lizzie nods. "But how do we get inside? What do we do when we're in there? And how do we get out again?"

I go back to Google and there's a new article there, posted by a recruitment site. The words *Stowerling Keep* have been highlighted by the search engine.

"Lizzie!" I point. "They're looking for extra staff for this weekend."

"No freaking way!" Lizzie leans forwards. "No *way* is Gold hiring from outside."

"Serving staff and cleaners." I grin. "*Cleaners*, Lizzie, for this weekend."

"We can hardly apply for the job." Lizzie sighs.

"I know, but if we find the right place to wait, someone who did apply for the job is bound to go past. If we offer them enough money, they'll swap with us. What do you think?"

"I think he'll have surveillance everywhere. We'll be seen. As soon as he realizes it's us, we're dead."

"You don't look much like you used to."

"Facial recognition," she says. "He's bound to have it. And there's gait recognition too."

"Then we'll have to change our faces." I pick up the phone. "See what you can find online to help us while I text Grady. I want to see if he knows what's at Stowerling Keep."

After a moment Lizzie nudges me. "I'm going to need some decent make-up. I might be able to change our looks enough with contouring. You can wear your fringe over your face too. It's long enough now."

I touch her hand. "What about the way we walk?"

She turns her hand to hold mine. "Apparently there's nothing we can do about that. I thought I could put inserts in our shoes or something, but it won't fool the technology. The only thing on our side is that the tech isn't real-time yet, so Gold might not have it installed." She finally looks at me. "Has Grady replied?"

I show her the phone.

Corporate team bonding

She frowns. "He doesn't believe that."

"It'll be like the island."

Lizzie fixes her gaze on her phone. "We don't have to go, Ben. I know you told Grady we'd help him…"

"It's not about helping Grady. It's about showing the world who Gold really *is* and what he does to kids like us. It's about getting justice for Will and all the others who died on the island. It's about—"

"Going home," she finishes for me.

"Getting you home," I correct her. "I'm in no hurry to get back to Mum, and Dad has his

45

new family … but you need to see your parents and we have to get you to a doctor for your headaches and dizziness."

"Are you really willing to risk your life for that?"

I resist blurting out that I'd do anything for her. "It's worth the risk," I say instead, without looking at her.

"I can't be responsible for…" She tails off, then she pushes her chair away from the desk and abruptly stands. "If something happens to you, it'll be because of me. Again."

"Why because of you? This is my choice."

"But you're doing it for *me*."

"For *us*." She's going to run. I grab her arm. "What kind of lives are we facing? Hiding out here was only ever a short-term solution. How will we survive beyond this? If something happens to Grady this weekend, we won't be getting any more money from him. Those fake IDs aren't up to *that* much. We can't claim benefits, we can't go to uni, we can't get proper jobs." I pull her into my chest. She resists at first, then melts into me with a small sob. "Lizzie, if we take down Gold, we can get our lives back. If we don't do this, if Grady dies, he won't be able to send any more money. And you'll never be able to see your parents again."

"Dad thinks I'm dead." She shudders with sobs. "Is he even fighting any more?"

"Of course he is." I stroke her back and I feel my own head growing fuzzy, a tingling behind my eyes. Those damn pills. "If we do this, you could be back with him by next week. Imagine how he'll feel when he finds out you're alive."

"If it's like Aikenhead, we could both end up dead."

"I won't let anything happen to you." I hold her tightly. She knows it's a promise I might not be able to keep.

"So, we're going to Scotland?" Lizzie raises her head. Her lips are close to mine. I want to kiss her so badly, but I don't think *she* wants that. My head thumps again. I've always had migraines, but these are something else. My vision blurs.

"We're getting into Stowerling Keep," I tell her. "But we're not going in blind this time. We're taking weapons, a decent medical kit, cameras and anything else we can think of that might protect us. We'll record everything that happens, and if we can't send the file to Matt while we're there, then we'll leave with the rest of the staff and do it afterwards." I'm finding it hard to think. "Isn't there a beach behind the castle? We'll buy a kayak when we get to Scotland and hide it in the sand, just in case."

Lizzie's shoulders tense. "We just have to make sure that Gold doesn't realize we're there, because if he does, he'll never let us leave."

Chapter Seven

Grady

The car pulls into an enormous forecourt. The castle itself glows in the early afternoon haze. A fountain sparkles and the manicured lawn is like an emerald carpet. There are dozens of windows, all reflecting the setting sun. There are two turrets. One of them has a balcony running round the outside.

Aanay has hardly said a word all journey.

"Take a look." I point but Aanay just shrugs.

"It's only material wealth, Grady," he says.

"Time to get out, gentlemen." There's a click as the chauffeur unlocks our doors. We have no choice. He won't take us back to London and anyway, if I don't enter the castle, there's a video of me that will simultaneously hit the police, social media and all the news stations.

"Please leave your phones on the back seat," the chauffeur says, and I pull mine out of my pocket. It doesn't matter if Gold gets hold of it, it's not the burner I've been using to contact Ben and Lizzie. There's nothing on this one but a few games and some chilly messages from my father. I'm sure someone will enjoy analyzing those...

Abandoning my phone, I step on to the crunching gravel, my eyes going to the other cars that are parked in a rough semicircle around the driveway. Three other limos. I wonder who else is here. Who else has earned the pleasure of 'corporate team bonding'?

There are wide stone steps that lead up to a carved wooden door. The chauffeur hands me my bag, which has obviously been emptied and repacked. It's lighter than it was when I handed it to him in the city. I guess I'm missing my weapons, painkillers, stimulants and electronics. I imagine even the small gas mask will have been removed. Oh well, it was worth a try.

He points the way and I resist squinting into the dark woodland between the thick tree trunks and into the green undergrowth. I shouldn't try to spot Ben or Lizzie. I don't know their plan; I don't even know if they've made it here. I can only *hope*. Because if I'm going to die this weekend, and I really don't intend to, then I want to know that Gold is going down with me.

My feet hardly make a sound on the stone steps. I'm wearing sneakers, black so they look like shoes, but much more sensible if I have to run. Aanay is right behind me, his breath coming in short gasps. He's terrified. If he's going to be any use to me, I'll have to calm him down. I turn. "I want to keep my hands free. Will you—?"

"Carry your bag for you?" Aanay takes it from me.

"I don't know what we're going to face in there." I pull off my glasses and tuck them into my top pocket. The glass in them is easily broken; that's a weapon they missed, right there. I start to smile. "I'm going to look out for you, if I can. All right?"

"Why?" Aanay's brows tuck together in a frown. "I saw that picture. I know you're not like me. You're like *them*." He's thinking of the clones.

My smile is cold. "Because I choose to. They don't get to dictate who I am, who lives or dies at my hand." I pin him with my stare. "They won't want me to live through this and they won't want me to help you survive. So I will."

"I'm your middle finger up to the man." Aanay's mouth twitches.

"If you like."

"I thought you were like me," Aanay said, not moving from the step. "Until I saw that photo. You didn't even seem to care about that girl."

"Carmen," I say, rolling her name around my mouth. "She was so damaged by the time we'd reached the end, mentally as well as physically. What I did was a kindness. Anyway, you killed your *sister* to get here." I lower my voice.

"She ran on to the knife I was holding." Aanay's cry is anguished. "She killed herself after Gold demanded a death." He looks at me. "I'm only here because I was the last one standing. I think our cousin's friend, Nadia, was the one who was meant to get through, but Dhaval and Nadia died when someone cut the ropes they were climbing."

I look at the dark wood of the door above us. "Gold knows this?"

Aanay nods. "He said I had to join the programme anyway. He has a plan for me." He touches my arm. "You know that my family is Jain – he wants me to become a religious leader, an influencer under his control." Aanay drops his hand. "He doesn't know enough about it, though. Becoming a Jain ascetic requires permission from my parents and they'd never give it. They know me. They know that I don't have the courage or determination to embrace Jain *deeksha*." He shrugs. "I have my beliefs, and they're important to me, but I also watch Netflix and play football. I liked gaming at Dhaval's house — we did escape rooms once a month." He looks at his feet. "Our local venue used our group to test out their new scenarios." He swallows. "When I found out what he wanted from me, I thought about killing myself, but he said if I die by my own hand, my parents will see a video of Indrani's death."

"Which you say wasn't your fault."

Aanay's smile is bitter. "I was holding the knife, Grady. I'd stolen it from another team. That's *theft*, which means I broke one of my *mahavratas*."

"*Mahavratas?*"

"One of our five central vows. If I hadn't done that, Indrani wouldn't have died."

"Ah." There's a creak above us as the door opens. A man is standing in the doorway wearing a black suit and tie. He's old as time but standing straighter than anyone I've ever seen, like there's a rod down the back of his jacket.

"Gentlemen," he says. "Let me show you to your room."

We follow him into the building, and I stand motionless, taking a moment for my eyes to adjust to the dimmer light.

"To your right is the main entrance hall." The man points with one gnarled finger. "You have come in through the garden entrance. The door down those steps is the original, made by a British craftsman in 1675. It is worth a closer look once you're settled."

It seems as if we're getting a tour.

"Just in front of you and to your right, you can see the dining room. You are expected there at six for aperitifs. Dinner will be served at seven. Please dress accordingly." He sniffs towards my shoes. I ignore his expression and look up. As I had expected, there are cameras: lenses in the ceiling, one above each door frame, small red lights following our every move.

"We are opposite the kitchen," the old man continues, and I notice that every door is solid oak – and with a keypad beside it. If I can barricade myself into a room, there'll be no getting through. I smile again. Then he starts walking. "And now we are in the gallery. Some of these works of art are hundreds of years old and they are all originals."

I glance sideways. There are a number of paintings on the walls. We're walking too fast to get a good look, but I spot a still life, a cooking tableau, a woman hanging out clothes, all very domestic. My eye is caught by a large religious scene. As I said, I prefer Cubism, but... "I've seen this one before," I muse, stopping in front of it and examining the image. There's a robed bearded man holding down a screaming boy by the throat and face. He has a knife and is preparing to use it. It was the boy's expression that had captured me when I visited Italy. The open mouth, the terror and betrayal in his eyes. I'd liked it very much.

"It's quite famous," the old man says.

"You said they were all originals. This is a copy."

The old man smirks. "Actually, the one hanging in the Uffizi is a forgery."

I am about to say that it can't be true. That Gold can't have an original Caravaggio hanging in his hallway, I could reach out and touch it, there's not even any security, but then I close my mouth. Why *wouldn't* he have something like this? The man is powerful enough, rich enough, he could easily have arranged the swap.

The old man points to the frame next to the Caravaggio, it contains a map of the castle. "In case you get lost," he says.

Aanay stares at it. "Music room, library, armoury." His finger traces the lines. "There are children's rooms upstairs." He sounds surprised. "And a chapel."

"Mister Gold raised his family here, at least part of the time." The old man sniffs. "Three girls and a boy. Home-educated, as you can see. There's a classroom upstairs."

The old man has nothing more to say, he simply points to the left. We're obviously meant to keep walking. We stride through squares of light and dark, patches of sunlight brought in by the windows that line the gallery. My sneakers squeak on the parquet floor and the air smells of furniture polish and mouldering material. We pass a set of stairs to our right and then...

"Servants' quarters," Aanay reads. There's a plaque on the door.

"There's a lift in front of you, should you need it." He sneers as if, despite his age, he's never used it in his life. We turn a corner and he stops. "You are in guest bed one." He points. "You'll be sharing. The room has its own bathroom."

"Why are we sharing?" There's a second guestroom next to ours. "Who else is here?"

The man says nothing, simply unlocks the door with a key from the ring on his belt and walks away, swaying gently as he rounds the corner.

"Well, here we are." I open the door. The guestroom is large and has two beds. There's a wardrobe against one wall and a small bathroom. The wall displays more priceless art, another religious scene, the crucifixion this time. Jesus is screaming.

There's a camera above the frame, angled so that it can view the whole room. The window, when I walk to it, gapes into the woodland. The trees are so dense that despite the sunlit afternoon little light makes it into the room. A spider is spinning a web against the frame. Its fat abdomen rises and falls as it scuttles, dragging a silk line behind it. A fly is already struggling in the top corner.

"Which bed would you like?" Aanay lifts my bag.

"I don't mind." I put my hands behind my back. "I don't think we'll be getting much sleep anyway."

Aanay puts my bag on the bed nearest the door and I nod.

"How long till six?" I ask.

Aanay looks at his watch. "We've got an hour. Should we change and then explore?"

"Grady, I want to use the shower." Mother's voice is as soft as usual, even though she's been waiting for half an hour. Even though she's going to be late for her dinner with Father and that will annoy him. I'm watching a spider in the bathroom. It's eating a wasp.

I had always wondered if the webs would be strong enough to trap something so powerful and sleekly dangerous. The wasp has been struggling for a while, but it's stopped now, and the spider's legs are wrapped around it.

"Grady, please." She puts a little emphasis on the please. There's a silent addendum. You know what your father's like.

She can't be late to dinner and she can't go without being freshly washed. It's a conundrum, for sure. I keep watching the spider.

Finally there are footsteps on the stairs, heavy ones. I hear Mother's slight gasp.

"What's going on?" Father's voice. He's grown tired of waiting, or perhaps he came upstairs to get his cufflinks from the bedside table and found Mother in the hallway, wringing her hands.

"Grady's in the bathroom," she says. "I'm sure he'll be finished soon."

"You're not even washed?"

Her intake of breath. "I'll be ready by the time we have to go; we won't be late."

There's silence and then the bathroom door is slammed open. Father stands, arms folded, staring at me. "What are you doing?"

I point. He looks with me at the dying wasp for a long moment. Then he lifts my hand and uses my palm to smash both spider and wasp.

I feel a sting in the centre of my hand.

"Now get out," he says.

▼

I lead Aanay slowly through the armoury, which, not unexpectedly, contains suits of armour. The swords look quite blunt, but there's a long spear that appears pleasingly sharp. I stand under the camera, which swivels to watch me, and reach up to touch the hilt. I pause when the tinkling sound of a piano drifts through the door marked *Music Room*.

Aanay looks at me nervously.

"Shall we find out who we're 'team bonding' with?" I ask him, dropping my hand. I can pick up the spear later.

He swallows. "I don't think I'm ready."

"Will you ever be?" I'm already walking towards the door. It's heavy and I have to lean on it with my shoulder to open it.

Bella Russo is sat by the piano. Her eyes are closed and her fingers flicker across the keys. A dangling silver necklace sways with her movements. I think it may be the first time I've ever seen her not consciously posing. There's pure pleasure on her face. She looks more beautiful than ever.

She isn't alone. Dawson King is leaning against a corner staircase that leads up to the first floor.

He is watching her possessively, with one hand in his pocket, gripping that notebook. He's noticed me looking at her and he isn't pleased. He flushes and clenches a fist as I step forwards. Then I realize there's a third person here, sitting at a small table, her ankles crossed in front of her: Iris. She isn't listening to Bella's playing, instead she is looking at her fingers with a slight frown.

"Evening, all." I let the door slam behind Aanay and there's a discordant note. Bella stops playing as if her hands have been smacked.

Dawson straightens. "I might've known you'd be here."

I move further into the room and Aanay is forced to emerge from behind me. "What did you to do to get sent here?"

"Team bonding, innit," Dawson says. "We've got to *bond*." He grins towards Bella and I sigh.

"You aren't that naive." There's a small sofa in the corner by the fireplace. I let myself sink into the creaking cushions and the scent of leather polish.

"What do you mean, Grady?" Bella frowns and turns round on the piano stool. I stare at her. She returns my gaze and her quizzical expression doesn't crack. She appears to be serious.

"This will be another test, like the one you took to get on the programme," Aanay explains gently from his position by the door.

"Test?" Bella shakes her head with a tinkling laugh. "There was no *test*." She examines her fingernails. "Marcus Gold bought my father's winery. After he met me, he offered me a job and Father insisted I take it." She doesn't sound very happy about that last part.

"You mean … you didn't have to…" Aanay trails off and slinks across the floor to stand beside me.

"Have to what?" Bella frowns and leans forwards. "What was your *test*, Aanay?"

"You don't need to answer her," I say to Aanay quickly. But he shakes his head.

"*Truth*, Grady." He looks at Bella, his eyes damp and serious. "My cousin Dhaval asked my sister and me to join his team for the Iron Teen competition, you might have seen it in the news?"

Bella frowns slightly as if she is trying to remember.

"Indrani and I didn't care about the money, but we thought it would be … fun." His voices tails off. "It wasn't fun. We had to fight for our lives." He stops again. "I broke vows. Dhaval died. His … friend, Nadia. My sister."

"All right, that's enough, Aanay." I touch his shoulder. The room feels smaller than it did, the red wallpaper, patterned with gold swirls, is making me feel nauseous. "I know *I'm* here as a punishment."

"Well, *I've* done nothing wrong," Bella snaps and she raises her arm, sweeping it across the room. "Does this look like a gladiator arena to you? We're here to have dinner and tomorrow we'll be paintballing in the woods or something, you ridiculous boy."

Dawson puts a hand on her shoulder. It's odd seeing him without the rest of the clones. His hair is darker than I'd thought it was, curling over his collar. His eyes are shrewd, his muscles bulge under his dress shirt. He is wearing it with the sleeves rolled up and for the first time I realize there's a tattoo curving around his right forearm. It's a crown: Dawson *King*. I roll my eyes.

"It *will* be a test, Bells," Dawson murmurs. "Chris warned me."

She stiffens and pulls away from him. "Why

would *Christopher Gold* warn *you*?"

"He's a mate." Dawson looks at me. "I didn't test into the grad scheme either. Chris got me in."

"*Chris?*" Iris looks up with a snap of her chin. "Christopher Gold doesn't have *friends*. Why would he do that?"

It's the most I've ever heard Iris speak. I look at her carefully. Christopher Gold seems to be some kind of trigger for *three* of the people here. Interesting.

"Saved his life." Dawson shrugs. "Bar fight. He pissed off the wrong people. Lucky I was there, really."

"So, Christopher Gold." I lean back. "You saved his life," I gesture to Bella. How best to provoke her? "You're his … side piece."

"I am no such—"

I ignore her and look at Iris. "And you?"

"I have nothing to do with Christopher Gold," Iris snaps, her cold eyes flashing with sudden fire.

"O-K." I draw out the word and she narrows her eyes at me.

Dawson squeezes on to the piano stool beside Bella. "I'll protect you, Bells." He puts an arm round her. "No one's going to hurt you."

"No one is going to hurt *anyone*." Bella shoots to her feet and heads for the door. "You are all *ridiculous children*. Children, playing stupid games. Christopher wouldn't send me anywhere *dangerous*! I'm going to the dining room." She slams out of the door leaving the four of us to stare after her.

"I think she's serious," Iris says eventually, smoothing down the skirt of her silk dress. It is the same cobalt-blue as her eyes. "She truly believes this is nothing more than a team-bonding weekend."

"And you?" I tilt my head.

"I know Gold." Iris looks back at her hands and then up again. "And you're right, of course. I assume he has videos of you both?"

Aanay nods and I allow my chin to dip in acknowledgement. Dawson holds up a hand. "Me too. That bar fight *might've* gone a bit far. He bought the surveillance."

"You killed someone?" Aanay's eyes are wide. "In a bar fight."

Dawson's answering grin chills even me. "Slit his throat. Want to know how it felt?"

"No, we don't." Iris shuts him down. "So, we know why Bella is here then."

"Why?" Dawson looks at her now.

"Gold needs a video."

"Of her killing one of us," Aanay says, and I have to admire his total commitment to honesty.

I nod. "I'm here because Gold doesn't trust me. I believe Aanay is here as a test, to see how far Gold can push him, if he can make him break his vows. Bella is here because Gold needs a video of her. Dawson … I don't know. Why *are* you here? I thought you were well in with the clones."

Dawson laughs at my terminology. "I *am* well in."

"Then why?"

"It's Dad." Dawson curls a lip. "Ian King, crown prince of crime or what have you. Gold's testing my loyalty. Am I his … or Dad's?"

"And which is it?" Iris frowns as she examines him.

Dawson shrugs. "Either, *both*. If I get a promotion and a Gold International company to run it'll be good for Dad. Money laundering, smuggling, I can do it all, but it'll look legit."

"I don't think Gold would like that." Aanay is so tense he's shaking. "His companies have to at least *seem* above board, right?"

"Right." I lean back. "You let your dad use your company and get caught, it puts Gold International under scrutiny."

Dawson shrugs. "It's the only way Dad would let me go."

"Let you go?" Aanay frowns.

"I'm his enforcer. Have been for a couple of years now. If he thinks I'm not doing something to benefit him, he'll call me home."

"You're between a rock and a hard place." Aanay sounds almost sympathetic.

"I've got good balance." Dawson's smile is bright and slightly crazy. I'm starting to think that he isn't psychopathic. Not like I am, not like the clones. He's too emotional and he's obviously got a crush on Bella. He might be a sociopath. Maybe that's another reason for Gold to test him.

I look at Iris. Now *she's* a psychopath. "Why are *you* here?"

Her eyes meet mine steadily. "None of your business," she says coldly.

There's a clear ringing sound. A bell. The old man appears in the doorway. "Dinner is about to be served."

Chapter Eight

Grady

The first thing that strikes me as I enter the dining room is the heat. There's a roaring fire blazing under a carved stone mantel bigger than most bathrooms. The long table in the centre of the room is set for five, with an ice bucket for each of us. Three huge windows dominate two of the walls, with sunset views out over the woodland on one side and cliffs on the other.

On either side of the fireplace there are tapestries, displayed against the pale gold wallpaper. One shows medieval villagers trying, and failing, to put out a fire. The seamstress had apparently enjoyed sewing all the little details on the burning peasants. The other depicts a battle scene more suitable for the armoury than the dining room. Blood and gore are strong themes. Aanay refuses to look at either of them; he sits facing the windows, his back to both.

Coats of arms on shields of different shapes hang

in the remaining wall spaces. The camera I'd expected to find is inset beside the glittering chandelier, its red light a contrast to the shards of bright white that gleam from crystal. There are four more smaller lenses, three in the corners and one above a second door that I assume leads into the kitchen. They squint down on each of us.

The only other furniture is a couple of dark wooden sideboards. The others are already sitting, but my attention is caught by the blond girl holding the water jug and another ice bucket. She has a thick fringe over the side of her face, make-up that sharpens her cheekbones, narrows her nose and thickens her brows, and her hair is tied loosely into a spiky ponytail. She is thin and her eyes are watering. *Contact lenses*, I think, *and she isn't used to them*.

She's wearing a Gold International cleaning uniform with a garish pin on her chest. A cleaning uniform, when she's serving at table? And who let her wear that hideous brooch? I inhale sharply. *Lizzie!* She looks utterly different. Instantly my shoulders start to descend. I wonder where Ben is.

I drag my gaze away from her, knowing that if I stare too long someone will wonder why. I make myself look only at the other four 'graduates' sitting around the table with me.

Bella is still not talking to us. She sits stiffly, refusing to look at Dawson, who is attempting to make her laugh by telling a story about his cousin trying to smuggle drugs through Heathrow in a teddy bear.

"He's doing seven-to-ten now." Dawson slaps his thigh as if this was the funniest thing he'd ever heard.

"He's insane," Aanay whispers and I nod.

Iris pushes her food round her plate, eating nothing. I look at my own chicken dinner with a frown. I need to keep my strength up, but could the food be drugged, poisoned? I glance at Lizzie, as though she might give me a clue, but she has added another ice bucket to the centre of the table and is now pouring a glass of wine for Bella, while avoiding my gaze.

To eat or not to eat? Aanay is glaring at his own chicken in disgust. He'll be going hungry. Perhaps this is his first test – feed a corpse to the vegan and see if he'll eat it. Aanay won't be so easily broken.

I watch Dawson devour his meal. Bella is eating too, although not as quickly. Both seem fine but not all drugs are fast-acting. I lean back in my chair and slide my knife and fork together. I can manage twenty-four hours without food. It's just a fast; Mother did them all the time. Father had liked her to be slim.

The old man slips into the room and speaks briefly to Lizzie. She nods and leaves. He looks at us, skimming our faces as if memorizing them, then he follows her, closing the door behind him. After a short while, I hear multiple footsteps and short conversations in the corridor outside, then silence falls once more.

I raise my eyes to Iris. "The staff just left, didn't they?"

Her face remains passive, but her fingers tighten on her water glass as she nods.

Where are Lizzie and Ben? Did they manage to defy the codger and stay? Will they hide somewhere or sneak back in? Have they left me?

I loosen my collar; the fire is raking hot nails over my chest and face. Sweat pricks under my armpits. The ceiling camera zooms in on me, I can tell by the way its light narrows in on my face. I lick my lips. Somewhere, someone is operating the surveillance.

Are they in the house, or controlling it remotely? I tap my finger against my plate. If it's like the island, there'll be no signal out, which means they have to be on-site. But where?

There's a click from the door and I jump as metal grilles slam over the three windows. A projection of a clock appears on the wall above the fireplace, between the tapestries. I turn, trying to see the location of the projector, but nothing is obvious. The clock itself has no hour hand and no hours marked on the dial. The second hand is already ticking round.

"Welcome, graduates," Marcus Gold's voice booms through the room. The last time he spoke to me, he'd been demanding that I murder Lizzie and Ben. I brace. "Congratulations, you are all in line for a promotion. All you have to do to secure your preferment is ... leave the castle. I will be watching to judge your particular strengths and weaknesses, how you operate, and the companies you are given to run will reflect the skills you demonstrate. Make me proud." His voice fades.

Bella spins towards me, her face glowing. "I told you it was nothing bad. This is not just team bonding, it will get us a *promotion*!"

"Oh, Bella," I sigh. "Go on then, leave. That's all you have to do, right?"

Bella stands and clicks her way to the door. "No one is going to try and stop me?"

"Why would we?" I spread my hands. "He didn't say we were fighting for placements. Anyone who gets out wins, right?"

She looks uncertain.

"Seems a bit too easy?"

Bella walks to the door. Dawson starts to his feet and then stops. We all watch her.

She reaches for the handle, looks back at me and pulls. Nothing happens. She pulls again, harder. She re-evaluates, shakes her head then *pushes* the door. It doesn't budge. She steps back into the room. "I don't understand." She strides to the door that leads to the kitchen and repeats the process. "The doors are locked and there are bars over the windows." The rest of us haven't moved. "How are we supposed to get out?" She points up at the glowing clock projection. "And what does *that* mean?"

Iris says nothing. Bella sits back at the table. I look at Aanay. He is staring at the congealing chicken on his plate and his face is pale.

"All right then," I say when no one else seems ready to speak. "Our first challenge is to get out of this locked room. How do we do that? Any ideas?"

"I think I know what this is, Grady," Aanay whispers. "It's an escape room."

"A what?" I look at him in surprise.

"An escape room – you remember I told you I used to do them with my friends? We would have to solve a mystery, or maybe we were trapped in a computer game, or locked in prison, something like that. They give you one hour to solve all the puzzles and get out."

"Puzzles like what?" Dawson has one arm round Bella, but she's watching Aanay with narrowed eyes.

"You have to find clues," Aanay says, warming up. "So, perhaps there's a padlock and you must find the key, or a code you need to find to open a safe. Each thing you uncover leads you to something else until eventually you find the code or key that will open the main door and you're free."

"Were you good at these escape rooms?" Iris asks.

Aanay nods. "We would always get out with time to spare."

I finally push my plate away and get to my feet. "How do we know what to look for?"

Aanay shakes his head. "We just have to search the room, then what we have to do should become clear."

"We just … poke around until we find something?" Bella steps away from Dawson. "Should we work together?"

"For now, at least." I shrug. "There's nothing to say otherwise."

"It is *team bonding*." Bella casts a smile at Dawson. "This could even be fun, don't you think?"

"Just be careful," I say as she starts towards the nearest sideboard. "The puzzles on Aikenhead were…"

"What?" She turns to Aanay when I don't complete my sentence. "What were they?"

"Horrible," Aanay says. "They were horrible."

Bella hesitates. Then she bends to open the cupboard. To my surprise the unit opens to reveal a full bar.

"We can have cocktails while we work!"

Bella cries. "See, Marcus Gold *has* set this up to be an evening of entertainment."

Iris hasn't risen from her chair. Her expression is disdainful as she shakes her head.

Aanay tugs my arm. "I think the tapestry must have a clue in it, but its violence is … upsetting."

The fire is too hot for me to go nearer, so I peer at the left-hand tapestry from where I stand. "It's just people trying to put out a fire."

"Maybe it's telling us what to do," Dawson calls. He's holding a glass up so that Bella can pour vodka into it.

"You mean we have to put out *that* fire?" I gesture at the inferno in the fireplace and then at the table. "It's going to take more than a few buckets of ice to douse that."

"Well." Aanay looks almost pleased. "We could smother it with that awful tapestry."

"That 'awful tapestry' is hundreds of years old!" Iris snaps.

"Don't care." Dawson puts his glass down and goes to the wall. He yanks at the tapestry and it descends with a tearing sound and a cloud of choking dust. "And the other one?" He's already pulling at it.

He dumps it on top of the first. It lands in thick folds with a medieval knight glowering up at him from the uppermost crease.

Iris steps back from the grimy material. "You're really going to put those on the fire?"

"Yes." I feel a frisson of pleasure. "If he didn't want his priceless tapestries chucked in the fireplace, he shouldn't have built a roaring great fire and locked us in with them."

"Fine then." Iris goes to fetch a bucket of ice. "If we wet them, they'll be less likely to act as fuel."

Aanay and Dawson pour out the water jugs, while I tip out ice buckets and Bella empties a soda canister. Iris stands back, watching, arms folded.

When we're finished, the tapestries are soaked.

"OK, Grady. It's you and me." Dawson picks up one side of the first tapestry with a grunt. "These are heavy."

I hang back for a second, wondering if one of the girls will offer to haul the soiled textile into the fire. When neither does, I pick up the other side. Dawson's right, it's heavy, the dense material made even heavier by the liquid it's absorbed. I hold it to my chin and together we drag it nearer to the hearth.

As we approach, sweat breaks out on my forehead. My skin crackles.

Dawson's face is rosy with heat and he's squinting against the brightness. "One, two, three, heave?" he asks and I nod.

I lift the tapestry as high as I can and when Dawson calls, "heave," I take a step and throw it forwards. The material flies for a second and then settles over the top of the fire with a puff of soot and the sound of shifting logs. Almost immediately flames eat through the image, as if it's coming to life. The stink of burning wool fills the room.

"Quick, the next one," Aanay chokes.

Dawson and I race back for the second tapestry. We drag it to the fireplace at a near run. This time I shout, "heave," and we hurl it on top of the oddly animating embroidered flames.

There's a moment when we hold our breath, but finally the fire starts to suffocate.

"Are there any more soda canisters?" I turn to Bella. "What about in the other sideboard?"

She rifles through the bar. "There's juice. Tomato, orange…"

"Over here then." Dawson holds out a hand and Bella tosses a carton at him. He opens it and squirts it at the smouldering tapestry.

"There's more." She pulls out four more cartons. "One each."

We all take one, except Iris who simply steps further away, watching.

Aanay picks up the spare and we join Dawson in pouring sticky sweetness over the charred mess in the great stone fireplace. Eventually the pile collapses with a defeated hiss. There's surprisingly little smoke but the whole thing reeks.

I cover my nose. "Now what?"

"We look for a clue." Aanay steps nearer to the hearth, holding his arm in front of his face to shield it from the intense heat.

"You think there might be something up the chimney?" I ask.

"Maybe." Dawson points. "What's that on the back wall?"

I squint through the heat haze. "Holes. The back wall has a load of holes in it."

"Do they make a pattern?" Aanay steps closer. "Maybe it's a word, or a number."

"Not sure." I let out a groan. "Has anyone got decent shoes on? Mine are rubber, they'll melt in there."

Dawson narrows his eyes then steps on to the remains of the fire. The mantel is so high that he barely needs to duck. He flinches when the heat surrounds him and hisses as his soles slide on the smoking hangings.

He catches his balance and scrutinizes the wall. "They're different depths, different angles. It's obviously meant to be *something*, but I don't know what."

Aanay helps Dawson climb out of the grate.

"So, we keep looking around." I walk back towards the table. "Maybe the puzzle has something to do with these coats of arms. Can anyone see a pattern … or a message?" I stare at the images surrounding us – stags, dragons, crowns, swords.

Behind me Bella makes a frustrated sound. "I'm going to have a drink." She storms to the cabinet and pours herself a generous glass. "There's no ice left," she mutters.

Iris still hasn't moved from her place beside the table. "Maybe we aren't meant to get out of this room," she says abruptly. "Maybe we're supposed to just … stay here."

"And do what?" Dawson sneers. "Gold said we have to get out of the castle."

"Maybe he was lying. The shutters might come up in the morning." Iris sits down. "I think we should just wait and see."

Bella lifts her glass in a silent toast. "Gets my vote."

Dawson looks at her. "Don't know about you, darlin', but I think if Gold is looking for someone to run a company, he isn't after someone who'll just sit around until an answer presents itself. This is like a job interview – don't you want that promotion?"

"And don't forget that clock." I point. "It's obviously a countdown of some sort." It's already showing us that fifteen minutes have passed. "Do you really want to know what happens when it reaches an hour?"

"What do you think happens in an hour?" Bella tilts her head.

I look at her. She is leaning on the bar, one finger playing with the rim of her glass.

It is Aanay who speaks. "In Iron Teen he used poison gas."

"He's right. There's a decent chance this room is going to fill with gas in about forty minutes." I turn to Iris. "Do you want to be here if I'm right?"

She doesn't answer and I look at the wall again, trying not to feel pressured by the constant jerky movement of the second hand in my peripheral vision. "Could there be something *behind* those coats of arms?"

Aanay moves to stand beside me. "It's worth a look."

I reach for the nearest shield and close my hand round the bottom, just as Bella shrugs. "I need a straw for my drink." Then she sneers. "Look, Gold *is* saving the world after all, one piece of plastic at a time." She holds up a straw from the cabinet.

"What do you mean?" Aanay asks.

"The gold straws." Bella waves the one in her hand. "They're metal."

I drop my hand from the shield. "Metal?" I bite my lip. "I can't see Gold caring about saving the environment. Hey, Dawson, those holes in the walls – how big were they?"

Dawson's eyes brighten. "Good call, mate." He snatches a handful of the straws from Bella and

82

heads back to the fireplace then he climbs in and carefully pokes one into a hole. "It fits! Made for it." He starts putting straws into all the holes as we crowd around the hearth in a semicircle.

Even Iris joins us. "I can't quite tell what it—"

"Here." Bella pulls her necklace off. "Join the dots."

Dawson wraps the necklace round each of the straws and the shape of a shield appears.

"I *was* right." Even knowing I could die tonight, it's satisfying to be right, to be solving a puzzle and finding pieces slotting into place. "It's something to do with the shields."

Dawson backs out of the fireplace. "Which one do you want?"

Bella tilts her head towards her necklace. "It has three points at the top, see?"

"There are a few that look like that." I point at the nearest, it has a lizard on it. "Maybe we need all of them. There could be something on the backs, a message?"

Dawson strides to the shield, grips it and pulls. Nothing happens. "It's stuck to the wall, hang on!" He pulls harder and the shield lifts.

Suddenly there's a flash of metal and a spray of blood. Dawson howls, but he remains standing with his hands holding the shield an inch away from the wall. Then he sways and his legs buckle. He releases the shield, which snaps back on to its hook, and collapses. For a moment I can't work out what has happened and then I see the blood pouring from his stomach, turning his shirt crimson, soaking his trousers.

Aanay backs towards the far corner. "*Grady! Do something!*"

I don't know what he thinks I can do – I haven't told anyone that Father is a doctor or that he expected me to memorize anatomy texts since the moment I could read – but I find myself kneeling at Dawson's side, my knees in his blood. His face is white and clammy, and his fingers are fluttering over his wound as if he can hold it together.

"What happened?" Bella's voice pierces the ringing in my ears. "What *was* that?"

"A blade." Iris examines the wall. "See here." She points but doesn't touch. Now that I'm really looking, I can see a crack in the stonework: a line as thin as a knife edge.

I use two fingers to lift Dawson's shirt. The slice runs from one side of his stomach to the other. It's deep. I can see his intestines: they're being held in place by his shirt and belt. I curl a lip.

Aanay starts to retch but I ignore him. "Bella, your scarf."

There's a moment of hesitation and then warm silk is placed in my outstretched hand.

I wrap it securely round the wound, lifting Dawson briefly so that I can stretch it across his back. At least now his guts have a chance of remaining on the *inside*.

The scarf is immediately soaked through. Dawson is like one of those soft dolls, a cabbage-patch creature, ripped up and tossed aside. "I can't fix this without a proper medical kit. I need to sew him together." I sit back on my haunches.

"This is bad, innit?" Dawson whispers hoarsely. "I thought there'd be ... violence ... I mean that's how you get promoted in my world ... but..."

"You weren't prepared for this." I lick my lips.

We all stand for long minutes, watching Dawson, then Iris turns away. "We're wasting time. Obviously picking the wrong shield has consequences."

She walks round the room. "But how can we tell which is the right one?"

"How can you even *think* about that right now?" Aanay chokes.

Click, swish. I look up. Bella's shadow falls over me. She's holding the bottle of vodka in one hand. "I'll sit with Dawson, Grady. You help Iris."

For a moment I think about refusing, but Bella still believes I'm infatuated with her and, for now, that's how it ought to stay. I pull off my jacket and I wad it into a ball. "Press that against his wound. Try to stem the bleeding."

Iris is still walking round the room. Her shoes are practical, her dress flared so that she can move easily. I narrow my eyes at her. Iris came prepared for more than dinner. She knew, just as I did, that Gold would be testing us. Did she have her own turn on Aikenhead? Or was Gold running other test centres, perhaps in areas where disappearing teens wouldn't make the national news? Where was Iris from, really? There were no clues in her voice. She was a riddle and I was going to work her out.

"There are lines in the wall under every shield," she says eventually, stepping closer to the centre of the room. "It could be any of them."

Aanay is still curled up in a corner, as far away from Dawson and the splash of blood as possible. Bella makes no sound as she presses my jacket to Dawson's stomach. He's groaning, in agony. Above his head the clock is still counting down. I gasp when I realise that we have only fifteen minutes left... Fourteen. Iris was right; we've wasted time.

"Grady, I think you were correct," Bella says. "This is not just team bonding."

"No."

"On the plus side, those of us who get out will really *deserve* that promotion." She smiles as if she's made a joke.

"*If* we get out." Aanay's arms are wrapped round his chest and he is rocking from side to side. "Only *one* person was allowed to survive Iron Teen. Why would this be any different?"

Dawson's groans turn urgent and Bella cries out as he clutches her arm. He's pointing at the ceiling. We follow the line of his finger until it drops.

"You have to lie down ... to see it," he gasps.

The table looks more comfortable than the

floor. I push crockery off, and it makes a satisfying crash, congealing food splashing on the flagstones. Then I lie, looking upwards, the polished wood hard against my spine.

I close one eye and then the other. The ceiling is pale beige, but it's an old house, the paintwork isn't smooth and when the light from the chandelier hits it… "It's a stag's head, isn't it?"

"Let me look." Iris lies beside me, her head close enough to mine that I can hear her breathing. "It *is* a stag," she says after a moment.

Finally, Aanay rises. "I'll count how many of the three-pointed shields have stags on," he whispers. He starts round the room and eventually stops at my feet. "There's only one."

"That must be the right one then." I roll off the table and glance at the clock. Nine minutes. I clench my fists. "Who's going to get it?"

Iris snorts and Bella looks at me with artfully wet eyes. "You can't ask me to do *that*, Grady. My hands are covered in Dawson's blood."

There's *no way* I'm pulling a shield off the wall. I look sideways at Aanay.

Aanay looks into my eyes and offers me a small

smile. Then he walks to the wall. "You're sure this is the right one, Grady?" Eight minutes.

I say nothing.

Aanay looks at the shield for what seems like an age. Seven minutes. "It follows the rules," he says finally.

"What rules? How can you say that there are *rules*?" Bella gestures at Dawson.

"Escape-room rules," Aanay says. "We found the clues. They led us here. If this isn't the right shield, then it's *cheating*." Six minutes.

He grabs the shield in both hands. He has to reach above his head to do it. If he's wrong, if the blade comes out of the wall, his throat will be cut. He yanks. The shield jerks away from the wall so easily that Aanay falls backwards and crashes to the ground, still holding tightly to his prize.

Hanging on a hook behind the shield is a small torch.

"It's not a key. It's not the way out," Bella breathes and her disappointment matches my own.

My eyes are pulled back to the clock. Five minutes. My lips are suddenly dry. I pull the torch from the wall and switch it on. It casts a faint pale blue light on to the table. "It's not a real torch. What use is this?"

"It's a *UV* torch." Aanay picks himself up. His eyes flicker nervously to the clock and then back to me. "We'll probably need it later. Don't lose it."

I slide it into my pocket. Iris's eyes don't leave my hands.

"Now what?" Bella's voice is pitched higher than usual. Four minutes.

Aanay smiles his small smile at her. "Don't worry, Bella," he says, handing me the shield. "I found the key."

"Where?" I look down at the curved metal, warm in my hand. There's a key stuck under the leather strap at the back. I pull it free and drop the shield with a clang.

"Which door do you think it opens?" I look at the others. "What happens if we try the wrong one?"

Aanay shrugs. "Maybe nothing? Or …" He tails off. Three minutes.

I head towards the main door, examining the key. It seems too small, incongruous against the huge portal. I shake my head and turn to the other, which has a step leading up to it. I climb and slip the

90

key into the lock. "Here goes." Two minutes.

I turn it and there's a click. I put my hand on the handle, take a breath and push. The door opens. For a moment I see a darkened kitchen illuminated only by the dining-room chandelier and the orange light filtering through a single window. The blended scents of our dinner and recently used cleaning products waft around me. Then, behind me, the dining-room light blinks out, the clock vanishes, and we're plunged into darkness.

"Grady!" Aanay sounds panicked and I quickly shut the kitchen door. Immediately the dining-room light crackles back on, one gleaming candelabra at a time, and the clock returns, showing one minute left. It starts to tick.

"I guess the rooms only operate with the doors closed. We can't leave this one open behind us." I gesture towards Dawson. "Should we leave him here?"

Dawson himself answers with a groan. "It's a kitchen. There could be a ... first-aid kit." With fascinating agony, he rolls to his feet, clutching his stomach in clawed hands. I realize that we are all watching him, no one moving to help.

We have thirty seconds left.

Aanay rushes to slip his shoulder under Dawson's.

When everyone is gathered round the step behind me, I glance at the clock again: five seconds. I open the door once more. The lights blink off, the clock shuts down and this time I step into the darkened kitchen. There's a window above the sink and enough light slinks between the bars to let me find my way safely inside. When we are in, I pull the dining-room door closed behind us. The kitchen lights come on with a fluorescent hiss, a new clock is projected on to the wall and Dawson collapses.

"I guess we're doing this all over again," I say looking at the clock.

"*Grady!* Is that you?" There's a terrified shout from the door directly opposite us.

Lizzie. It looks like they managed to stay in the castle after all.

She's trapped in the room on the other side of the kitchen. There's a sign on it: *Pantry*. There's nothing I can do. She'll have to find her own way out.

Chapter Nine

Ben

It cost me five hundred pounds of the £100K Grady had given us, to pay off two of the temp staff who were meant to be here tonight and, for now, my name is Tony McKenzie. Lizzie is Laura Fisher. No one has questioned our presence.

When we arrived, Lizzie was co-opted as a server. I was put on washing-up duty. It galled to know that I was washing dishes for Gold and that Lizzie was serving Grady like he was Lord of the Manor. Every time I think of him, I also think of Carmen, the feel of my friend's blood on my hands as I tried to staunch the bleeding, the terror in her eyes as she died in Will's arms. I think he'd loved her, so far as he was capable of it. Her death changed something in him.

"Don't think about it," I mutter. "But you *have to* think about it. *Don't* forget Carmen, Grady will only help you survive this if it benefits him." I catch my reflection in the copper side of the pot I'm scrubbing, my hair is flopping into my eyes. "Hello, Will," I whisper. "I wish you were here."

The chef is looking at me sideways and the camera in the ceiling feels as if it's trained on my shoulders. The hair on the back of my neck stands up. I jump as Lizzie claps me on my back. I've been standing still for so long, staring into the pot, that the water has gone cold around my hands. I pull them out of the water and stare at my fingertips. They were wrinkled and itchy. They'd been fine a moment ago. Hadn't they?

"Mr Matthews wants us to leave," Lizzie is saying. "*Everyone* is leaving."

The chef and his two assistants are already untying their aprons and heading for the door; the camera in the corner of the room whirrs as it traces their movements. The younger one looks back at me. "Come on, Tony. You don't want to be here in five minutes!"

"Why?" I give him a frown. "What happens in five minutes?"

Lizzie steps closer to him, making sure her camera-brooch is facing his lips.

"Just get a move on," the chef mutters, shoving his assistant out ahead of him as he flees.

Lizzie hisses her disappointment.

Other staff are converging from elsewhere in the house, I hear them in the corridor outside. The kitchen door closes, leaving just Lizzie and me.

"Did you have your 'accident' in the pantry?" she whispers as she hunches and pulls a tiny LED from her bra, palming it away from the kitchen camera.

I nod. It had been easy enough to trip on the cellar step, reach up for balance and 'accidentally' cover the red-eyed camera with a smear of the leftover pâté I'd been taking to the freezer.

"What if they get suspicious?" I take her arm. "The minute they realize something's wrong, Gold will send people in to extract us." To be honest, I've been expecting them all afternoon. My muscles are stiff from the constant anticipation of discovery and my mind has been screaming that this is a *mistake*. Lizzie's miserable, but at least she's alive. "I've changed my mind, Lizzie, I think we should leave."

It's not a mistake, we need revenge. The other voice in my head, the one I keep listening to when I shouldn't.

Lizzie puts her mouth to my ear. "We have to be

here to make our recording, Ben. We have to get proof of Gold's crimes, or our lives are over."

She's parroting my own words back to me, but we were wrong. Our lives would have gone on. They might not have been great lives, but there could have been great moments. We could have been together for as long as she'd stayed with me. Now she could be gone by morning.

We knew he'd have surveillance. The voice again. Of course we'd known. He'd put cameras all over an island, how much easier to watch a building?

We knew we might need to hide. Which is why I'd prepared the pantry as best I could. But I hadn't considered how quickly our game might be up. The moment we failed to leave the castle with the other staff, someone was bound to come looking for Tony and Laura.

"We have to *try*, Ben." Lizzie aims her LED at the kitchen camera, blinding it, and gives me a push towards the pantry.

What if there are other cameras we can't see? What if that camera is a dummy, just there to trick us?

I crash into the pantry door and hold it open for

Lizzie. She follows me, walking backwards, keeping her light trained on the lens. Then I let the door slam and we're inside, next to the bag we tucked under the pantry shelf with our coats when we arrived. I pull it out.

I hand the serrated knife to Lizzie, who slips it in the holster under her uniform skirt, but I keep the set of brass knuckles (it's amazing what you can buy online). I check the medical kit, rope and bolt cutters, I also open the sat phone I'd bought with a chunk of Grady's money. It's not working.

Lizzie looks disappointed but she shrugs. "It was worth a try."

"Right." I dump it back in the bag with the rope and sling it over my shoulder. "Ready?"

Lizzie swallows then she reaches up and slaps the light off. Darkness falls. We're hiding, waiting for everyone to go. Waiting for it to begin. Whatever is going to happen, we'll see at least some of it. Until they come for us, and then I'll fight like hell to give Lizzie a chance to escape with the recording.

We're going to get our revenge.

▼

Lizzie stares at her watch as the minutes tick by and then there's a loud click and something crashes over by the cellar steps. Lizzie grips my hand and my knuckles crunch together as she squeezes. Our breathing rattles in the enclosed space. Is this it? Has Gold found us? Nothing else happens and eventually Lizzie lets me go and stands up. She switches on her LED and I stare. Pitted metal bars have appeared over the cellar steps, completely blocking them off. With a frown, Lizzie pulls at the door to the pantry, but it doesn't move.

"We're locked in." The torch shakes in her hand. "How can we record what's happening out there if we're locked in here?"

"They must be coming for us." I reach past her and hit the light switch. "No need to sit in the dark any longer." The light comes on and, as it does, a keypad beside the pantry door lights up, I hadn't even noticed it the last time I was in here. I'd just assumed the pantry locked with a key. A clock also appears on the rear wall next to the cellar steps. It's being projected there; I follow the light back to the keypad by the door.

"What *is* that?" Lizzie stares. "It's not even telling

98

the right time." The second hand is ticking round, silently jerking towards the hour.

"How long, do you think, before Gold comes for us?" I wrap my arms round her. It's been a while since I last dared to pull her into a hug, her ribs dig into my chest. I put my nose in her hair. It still smells of her favourite shampoo: peaches and vanilla. It's home to me.

Lizzie doesn't take her eyes from the clock. The second hand has ticked all the way round and now the minute hand has moved too. One minute.

"Well ... there's a clock there." Lizzie shakes her head. "It would be just like Gold to torture us with some kind of countdown. Maybe he'll show when the hour is up."

An hour left to live. An *hour* left with Lizzie.

"If only I could have live streamed our recording ... the whole world could be watching what happens to us." Lizzie punches my arm in bitter frustration but, just like Aikenhead, Stowerling Keep is a dead zone. Gold isn't allowing unauthorized communications in or out of the castle.

"We can't just sit and wait for his people." She pulls away. "Let me try and get that door open.

If we can get out of here, we can escape through the kitchen window, get to the kayak we hid on the beach and try again another time." She looks at my face. "I'm not giving up, Ben."

"It's no good." I look at the keypad over her shoulder. "There must be thousands of possible combinations. What are the chances of getting it right?"

"Then we break through the door. Look for something we can use to smash it open. Something heavy – or sharp!"

"This is the pantry, Lizzie. There's only food." I pick up a packet of Bourbons and hand it to her. "Hey – you used to love these!"

She drops the packet on the floor then freezes. "Ben, there's a *number three* on the shelf. It was under the biscuits."

"A three?" My eyes flick from the shelf to the keypad. "What if the chef couldn't remember the door code? What if he wrote it down?"

"It's only one number," she says. "Are there more?"

We start dumping food on the floor, covering our feet with spilled flour, tins and packets, until we uncover four numbers. "That's a one, a three, a nine and a five." Lizzie cries triumphantly, stepping back.

"How do we know there're only *four* numbers in the code." I bite my thumbnail and Lizzie glares at me.

"We don't, I'll just try all the combinations and if they don't work, then we'll look for more. We're getting out of here! One, three, nine, five, right?" She taps in the numbers. Nothing happens.

"Press the enter key." I look over her shoulder. "Right there."

She presses it. There's a loud beep and the keypad flashes red. The door doesn't move. "Wrong n—" she starts and then her words die.

Something is hissing like a furious snake. I look down and, for the first time, see the vents around the bottom of the room and the sickly yellow gas curling up from them.

▼

"Ben!" Lizzie cried out and I looked round. A yellowish gas was spreading into the room from the edges of the floor.

"Hurry, Ben!" Will pulled his T-shirt over his face and

I saw Lizzie's pale stomach as she did the same. The gas rose insidiously, faster than I could have imagined, and I took a deep breath, trying to hold it as the gas started to fill the air.

▼

"*Lizzie!* It's like the island! Cover your mouth, quick."

She drops the torch and it shatters on the floor as she starts breathing through her fingers, her eyes wide and terrified. "He's gassing us!"

"It's automatic. It started when we put the wrong number in." I start shoving bags of flour under the shelves, trying to block the vents. Lizzie kneels to help, dragging a sack of rice and jamming it over the nearest outlet. She's coughing, trying to hold her breath. My own lungs are burning and my head swims. "We've got to get out!" I look up at the clock. Half an hour gone. How is that possible? There's no way that took us half an hour. I look at the keypad again.

The wrong number, somehow it jumped the clock too.

"Stupid, stupid, stupid." I'm muttering the word like it'll save us. "*Stupid! Stupid—*"

"Ben, stop!" Lizzie sobs. Her hands are shaking, her shoulders too. "I can't … this brings it all back … the island, it was…"

"I know." I grab her hands and hold them.

"You *hurt* me," she wails. "And then Grady killed—"

"I know, I'm sorry, I know."

What more can I say? I did hurt her.

"It's genetic, Ben," Will whispered. "If it's in Mother and me, it has to be in you too." He was so close now that his breath touched my ear, warm against my skin. "It's easy. It'll be like Lizzie's falling asleep. She's tired. Don't you think she's had enough of fighting?" His hands were across me now, reaching for Lizzie's throat. "Just don't think about what's happening. It's my turn to look after you."

If Grady hadn't picked that moment to stab Carmen and crow about his victory, would I have let Will choke the life from the girl I loved? Would I have continued to stand there and hold her while he did it? The shame that always lived, slippery under my skin, oozed through my pores, its rancid bitterness clogging my nostrils.

I'd told Lizzie I'd loved her on the island, screamed that I loved her when I found her body on the beach, but never since then. What if she didn't say it back ... or if she did, what kind of person did it make *her* if she could love someone as damaged as *me*?

"It's all right, Ben." Lizzie has her arms round *me* now and we're somehow holding one another as if we're both drowning and the other is a life buoy. "There's got to be a way out. We'll find it."

It's a game. Will's voice again as my head pounds. *It's all a game.*

"It's a game," I say out loud.

Lizzie frowns at me. "What do you—?"

"He's right, it's a *game*." I straighten up on to my knees. "Don't you see, Lizzie, it's like Iron Teen. Riddles to solve, codes to find, boxes to open."

"B–Ben." Lizzie's face is white. "There *is* a box."

"No." But I follow her gaze. A locked box is sitting under the far shelf. "That might not be part of this."

She sneers bitterly. "Of course it's part of this." Moving like an automaton, she pulls the box out from the shelf. It is just like the ones on Aikenhead, complete with the electronic touchpad on the top.

In the distance the lights of a cargo ship floated above the black water and the glimmering aura of the mainland town lightened the sky. The land behind us sloped subtly downwards back towards the estuary. I returned my gaze to the cairn, a pile of stones in a rough triangular shape. My torch showed a chain on the bottom linked to a metal box about the size of a lunch box, with a small black screen on the top.

Carmen clapped her hands. "Let's open this thing."

"And then we can eat," Grady said brightly.

Lizzie sat by the box and she pressed her thumb to the top. Immediately the screen lit up with the words:
WELCOME, ELIZABETH BELLAMY

Lizzie's lips are grey.

"Don't," I whisper. "Don't!"

As if she's dreaming, she puts her thumb on top of the box.

WELCOME, ELIZABETH BELLAMY

The curse is a faint whisper on my lips.

"He knew we were coming." Lizzie looks up at me, tears swimming in her eyes. "He knew all along." Her eyes are fixed to the box. Neither of us can look away.

"I can't open it," she sobs, her teeth chattering. "Not again."

Will opened the lid, then he looked at me. His eyebrows rose, ever so slightly. I'd never seen Will disturbed before.

"What is it, Will?" I tried to remain calm, but my mind was racing.

"What's in the box?" Grady yelled.

Wordlessly Will held up the small metal container for us all to see.

Inside, still bloody, with pieces of gum hanging off it and a corroded silver filling glinting in the torchlight, was a tooth.

"I think we have to." I slide the box out from under her hands. Using my thumbs, I carefully lift the lid. I can no longer hear Lizzie breathing. I flick the lid all the way open and stare.

There's no tooth. Instead we're looking at a book.

"It's a recipe book." Lizzie's words sink into the silence like stones. "I don't understand."

I pick it up gingerly. The gas is affecting my vision now; my eyes are swimming, everything tinged in garish yellow. My head pounds. I open the book.

There are dozens of recipes in here. Lizzie reaches past me and flicks from page to page. "Scones, Shrewsbury biscuits, tea loaf, tiffin … ordinary recipes."

The room is spinning and Lizzie looks watery, as if she really did drown back on the island. "We have to get up." I catch her arm. "We have to get away from the gas."

Lizzie lets out a giggle that is almost a burp. She looks shocked at herself but lets me pull her to her feet. The air is fresher and my head clears a little. I stare at the book again.

"Let me see." Lizzie turns to the contents page. "One of the recipes is marked," she says and she's right. There's a pencil mark next to one of the titles, a small AU.

"AU, what's that?" I frown and Lizzie shrugs.

"Someone's initials? The domain name for Australia?"

"The chemical symbol for gold?" I whisper.

She shivers. "What's the recipe?"

I read the words out loud, forming each syllable as if they're written in a foreign language. "Golden-syrup dumplings, page thirty-one."

"Find it." Lizzie thrusts the book back at me, and I turn the pages until I see the title I'm looking for. "Golden-syrup dumplings," I read out loud. "Ingredients: *butter, soft brown sugar, golden syrup, milk, self-raising—*"

"There was a number under the self-raising flour." Lizzie staggers sideways, her shoes crunching on the broken pieces of her torch. "It was the second one I found. It was the…" She pauses.

The self-raising flour is on the floor next to one of the shelves. There are a lot of ingredients on the floor. I look at the clock, another twenty minutes has vanished.

"Which number?" I look at the mess and at the shelf. "Which one was the flour?"

"The three?" She rubs her temples.

"No – that was under the biscuits."

"Then the one."

"Are you sure?"

"I'm sure. You found the nine and five, remember?"

I try, but my brain is fuzzy.

The golden syrup is still on a shelf, pushed to the back. I lift it up. "There *is* a number here. We missed it before."

"What is it?"

"A two."

Lizzie's eyes brighten. "We never looked in the fridge."

The giant fridge is by the door. Lizzie hauls it open with a grunt, snatches the butter out and tosses it on the floor. "Seven!"

I reach past her for the milk and drop it after the butter. "Four."

Lizzie grins. "We're doing this. Where's the brown sugar?"

I find it and hand it to Lizzie. "What's the number?"

"One again."

I nod.

"One, two, seven, four, one." She races to the keypad and is typing in the figures before I can stop her. She hits enter.

The keypad flashes red and there's a shrill beep that rings in my ears and sounds like the end of the world. Another set of vents opens near the ceiling and more gas filters into the room. The clock jumps another fifteen minutes. Our time is almost up.

Lizzie screams and punches the door. She leans her head against the wood then she straightens.

"*Grady!* Is that you?" She pounds on the door. "*Grady!* We can't get out. There's *gas* ... in here. *Grady!*" She starts coughing and turns wildly towards me. "I heard Grady in the kitchen. He can get us out!"

"I can't open your door. You have to work it out for yourself." Grady's voice is colder than I remember it.

He's not hiding who he is any longer.

"We'll have to try another combination." I go to the keypad. "How about the order the ingredients are given in."

"What's that?" Lizzie is coughing harder now and only the door is holding her up. I'm not quite as bad. I'm bigger than she is, the gas is taking longer with me.

"Butter, that was seven." I tap it in, there's a gentle buzz under my finger. "Soft brown sugar: one." I press the key, another buzz.

"The clock has almost ... run out." Lizzie is gasping for air, clutching her throat.

I have to focus. "Golden syrup: t–two." I punch it in. "Milk: four." I jab my finger down. "Self-raising flour: one." The keypad wavers in front of me as I stab the figure. To my horror there is no gentle buzz and I realize that I hit the four again by accident.

"Ben!" Lizzie screams hoarsely over the beep and a third layer of vents pops open, the gas in the room is so thick now that I can barely see what I'm doing. Lizzie collapses, falling face first on to the floor. I blink and realize that I'm on my knees.

Again, you loser.

"Again. Seven, one, two, four ... one." I jam my numb finger on the final key and hit Enter. This time I get it right. The keypad flashes green, there's a click and the pantry door cracks open. The vents in the wall slide closed. I crawl to Lizzie and grab her arm; she's barely conscious. I have to get her away from the gas. I want to carry her, but I can't get off my knees. I drag her through the pantry door and into the kitchen, breathing in a great lungful of clean air as soon as I can do so.

When I look up, I see Grady standing in the darkened kitchen, watching us from beside the sink. I'd never known eyes could look so cruel, until I met the *real* Grady Jackson.

Standing next to him is a skinny boy, almost as small as Lizzie is, wearing a grey suit that is too big for him. His hands quickly cover his mouth at the sight of us.

With them are two girls I've never seen before. One is holding a bottle of vodka loosely in her hand. The other is ice-blue, through and through. There's a boy too, lying on the floor. He's surrounded by blood.

The ice-blue girl steps forward. Her eyes are blue, her dress is blue, her lips are thin and flat, as if she's never smiled in her life. She curls them. "Who are you? And *why* didn't you leave with the rest of the staff?"

Chapter Ten

Grady

"You made it then?" It's hard not to look disdainfully down at my two ... not friends. But more than acquaintances. *Partners.* My two *partners* are lying on the floor, coughing their lungs out. Gas is seeping through the open pantry door and into the kitchen.

Iris slowly appraises at me. "How do you know the *staff*, Grady?"

"Not now. We'd better close that door before the gas gets in here. Damn it, Ben," I say as I kick the door closed. The kitchen lights immediately come back on.

Ben rolls on to his back and takes Lizzie's hand. Nothing's changed there then. But Ben looks ... like Will. I haven't seen him since the island. He's dyed his ginger hair and grown it into a style that is much more like Will's was. More than that, though, he's slimmer, harder edged, his eyes have something in them that wasn't there before. Something that I recognize.

▼

"His mum died." The father is speaking. The sons require an explanation, apparently.

"How?" One of the boys. A question most people would have thought but not asked. I tilt my head. How interesting.

"Will!" The father admonishes him but there's a feeling of futility in his tone, as if he knows his words will be ignored. So, the boy's name is Will.

"It's all right." My father this time, I'm the only one being kept out of this particular conversation, made to stand in the kitchen alone while they talk. "She killed herself. She was very fragile." He pauses and I know he's hanging his head, giving them his 'grieving widower' expression. "That's why we've moved here — to get away from the memories."

Memories! He means gossip, speculation. He hates that. "Grady found her, I'm afraid." He finishes with just the right twist.

And yes, I did. After he sent me to look for her, knowing full well what I'd find. I'd stared at her body for several minutes, searching for a feeling, before I called him.

The father replies. "I'm so sorry, Doctor Jackson, that's awful!"

I haven't heard the mother speak. I wonder if she's like mine was: subservient, terrified. He sounds perfectly normal, but this house is so clean. The only thing out of place that I've seen is a skateboard, leaning against the back door. The people here are afraid of making a mess. I step even closer to the door, interested in this new family.

"Call me Theo, please." My father, so magnanimous.

"Theo." Their father again. "Of course, we'd like our boys to look after Grady, help him find his feet. It's just that Will is—"

"Will is a wonderful friend." The mother this time. And no, she's not the submissive one. I've got close enough to the door now that I can see her back through the crack. She's tall and straight and her voice could cut glass.

"O-of course he is." The father. "But you know he's not … brilliant with new people."

"I'm standing right here." That must be Will. He steps sideways and I see the pieces of him. Short brown hair, cool grey eyes, firm jaw, thin lips, straight thick brows. He's younger than I am.

"Don't worry, Will, it's OK," his brother, Ben, says. I lick my lips and toe the door slightly so that I can see

115

more clearly. Ben is taller than Will, his hair is ginger, his skin pale, his eyes bright blue. He has the same brows as Will, the same jaw, but his lips are fuller and smile easily. He's older, old enough to be having a growth spurt and starting to develop acne.

"Ben will keep an eye out for both of them, won't you, Ben?" Their mother.

Ben's eyes flick towards her, amazement glittering in them like a nova. "You want me to watch Will and Grady?" He licks his lips. "You've never … I mean I have to look after Will … don't I?"

"Will first, obviously." Their mother waves a hand. The father is also watching her with narrowed eyes, suspicious. She waves a hand again, airily. Her nonchalance is as fake as Father's magnanimity. "The boy just lost his mother."

"And I don't need looking after." Will's voice is scornful. Ben pats his shoulder.

Their father looks at mine. "I'm not saying he can't be friends with Ben and Will, just that Will is…" He swallows. "There are a lot of other kids in the class he might be more comfortable with."

"Rubbish." Their mother grips Ben's elbow and propels him towards the door I'm hiding behind. "Take Will to the kitchen. Get Grady a drink. Don't make a mess."

"I'm meant to be meeting Lizzie at the skatepark."
With any other kid I'd have expected a whine to go
with the words, a plea, but Ben says it as if he knows
that arguing is pointless, he's just putting the information
out there.

"I want you to spend the afternoon with Grady," their
mother snaps. "Get to know your new friend."

Ben nods and guides Will towards the kitchen.

As they enter, I plaster a smile on my face. "Hey, guys!"
I point at the skateboard. "Is that yours? Did you know
that in the eighties the board manufacturers all got together
and decided they weren't going to use more than four colours
on any of their graphics, to save money?"

Ben gives me a wide, surprised, grin, Will stares at
me silently from his brother's side with a coldness in his
eyes that speaks to the chill writhing inside my own, as if
he can see through me, as if he already knows who I am.
He doesn't. He can't. I'm the new kid from down the road,
the most harmless person you'll ever meet. I smile more
widely. I'm a better chameleon than he is.

Their father sticks his face round the kitchen door.
"I'm just going to call Lizzie's mum and let her know
you can't make it this afternoon." He looks apologetically

at Ben. *"You boys all right?"*

Ben nods and so do I. Will just stands there staring. He really does have a lot to learn.

Ben goes to get us drinks and I lean back to look into the hallway again. Their mother and my father are standing close together, whispering-secrets close. I frown.

"And you're sure he wants the boys to be together?" she says.

"You saw the message." Father's voice is so low I can barely hear him.

"I don't like it." She glances towards the kitchen and sees me watching, listening. She grabs my father and moves them further down the hall. I turn back to see Will watching me with a half-smile on his face. I recognize the look. He thinks he's worked me out, solved the puzzle.

Then he speaks. *"What was it like when you found your dead mum?"*

I allow myself to gasp, let a tear into my eye, stagger backwards a bit.

"Will, no!" Ben is horrified.

I ignore the question, focus on Ben. Let myself stutter. *"W-what do you know about the illuminati?"* I begin.

▼

118

The kitchen has a single window and lets the cloudy twilight into the room through its bars. There are three exits. One leads back to the dining room, one to the pantry – where Ben and Lizzie came from. The other is the main door, which must lead back into the gallery.

"Anyone want to check that?" I gesture and Aanay tries the handle.

"It's locked."

No one is surprised.

Ben is shaking Lizzie, trying to get her to sit up. "Come on, Lizzie." He's coughing and wiping his mouth with his wrist. Lizzie's eyes are unfocused and she keeps slipping towards the floor, a doll with broken joints.

"I'll get her a glass of water." Aanay goes to the sink by the window and turns on a tap. Nothing happens. "It's not working."

"Yes, it is," Ben says. "I spent most of the afternoon washing dishes."

Aanay shrugs and turns the tap again. There's a distant clanking and then nothing.

Lizzie groans and grabs Ben's shoulder. Her eyes seem to be clearing. "My head!"

Ben digs into his bag. He pulls out a large medical kit, opens it and hands her painkillers. "Here."

"What are *those*?" Bella clicks her way towards them. "We need them." She waves towards Dawson with the vodka bottle. "What else have you got?"

"Mind your own business," Lizzie snaps. She tries to get to her feet but falls again.

Ben wobbles as he attempts to lift her. "A little help, Grady!"

With a sigh, I put an arm round Lizzie's shoulders and help her sit on a stool by the butcher's block. These two are meant to be helping *me*, not the other way round.

"What's happening?" Lizzie peers at me through bloodshot eyes. Ben's are the same, veins broken in the whites of his eyes; it must be the gas.

"And how do you know these people?" Iris repeats, folding her arms.

Moving like a snake, Bella snatches the medical kit from Ben. He jerks but doesn't stop her as she yanks out painkillers and bandages and tosses them to Aanay. "Here, make yourself useful."

Aanay stares between me and Dawson, his face pale. "It's all right, Aanay." I take the bandages from him. "I've got it." I kneel beside Dawson. Already the tiles are sticky with his blood. He's conscious but his eyes are closed. He opens them when he senses my presence.

"Can you dry swallow?" I hand him two pills and he gives a tiny nod. I lift his head and put them on his tongue; he chokes them down. I suppose it would be painful to watch, for someone else. I start to unravel the bandages.

"Have you got a suturing kit in there, Ben?" I gesture towards the first-aid kit.

"Yeah … I came prepared this time." He hands it down to me, and I thread the curved needle.

"We thought we were shut in there until Gold came for us." Lizzie leans on the butcher's block, her elbows almost touching the knives in the centre. She's speaking slowly. "But … this room's locked too? And … are the windows barred?" She puts her head on her forearms.

"I think all the rooms are going to be like this." I put the needle on a clean piece of padding and lay out the bandages. "Tell Ben and Lizzie what's going on, Aanay. I've got to concentrate."

I half listen to his explanation about escape rooms

as I remove Bella's scarf from Dawson's stomach. I unwrap him like a present as he whistles with pain, then I sit back on my heels for a moment, watching the blood throb from the wound.

"What's the problem, Grady?" Bella stands behind me.

"I need to sterilize this somehow, I—" I remember the bottle in her hand. "The vodka!"

Bella upends it over Dawson's stomach, and he howls as the liquid bubbles into and over him.

I bite back a snort of laughter and pick up the needle and thread. "Can you hold the wound together while I sew?"

Bella hesitates. I can see her running the risk-reward in her head, and the moment she decides there's no harm in helping me. In fact, it would be an advantage to have Dawson up, about and on her side. She kneels beside me on the floor. "What do I do?"

I pinch the skin together. It's thicker than you'd think, human skin, and feels almost rubbery. I show her where to put her fingers. "Hold it here, then move along the wound as I make the stitches." Dawson is writhing in agony now, his head thrown back. "Aanay, can you hold his shoulders?"

"I-I…" Aanay backs towards the sink.

"I'll do it." Ben is beside me, his familiar voice in my ear, his hand on my shoulder. Then he's holding Dawson, looking into his eyes. "It'll be all right, mate."

Dawson sneers.

"What happened to him anyway?" Ben's eyes gleam as he watches me, and I'm reminded of another question. *"What was it like when you found your dead mum?"* It was Will who had asked that, not Ben. So why did this feel the same?

"A blade came out of the wall," Bella announces as I stare at Ben, my mouth dry.

"Out of the wall?" Lizzie's head comes up with a jerk. "This is going to be worse than the island, isn't it?" She catches my eye. "Grady … Gold knew we'd be here."

I shake my head. "That's impossible."

Ben's hand wraps round my wrist; squeezes. "Did you tell him we were coming?"

"No!" I twitch. "He didn't know you were alive. He couldn't have."

Ben's grip tightens. "Then how did he know we were here?"

I wince and Bella touches Ben's shoulder. "If you break Grady's wrist, he won't be able to stitch Dawson up."

Ben releases me with a suddenness that makes me fall backwards.

"Who are you people?" Iris demands again, her foot tapping. "Why would Gold *care* that you're here?"

Lizzie looks at her steadily then sighs. "We were in Iron Teen ... with Grady."

Chapter Eleven

Grady

Aanay gasps and looks at me, there is accusation in his eyes. "You lied to me? You said you were the only survivor."

"I thought I was." I turn my attention back to Dawson, pick up the needle driver and use it like tweezers to clamp and lift the needle. I hold it between my fingers for a moment, thinking rapidly. "Ben and Lizzie swam for a passing boat. I didn't think they'd made it until Ben contacted me a few weeks ago."

"They couldn't ha—" Aanay sees my expression and stutters into silence.

Iris walks towards Lizzie, puts a finger on her chin, lifts her head. "Why are you here?"

Lizzie jerks free and stands on wobbling legs. "We're here to take down Gold. My friend died on that island. Ben's brother too. That man destroyed our lives."

Iris laughs. "Gold isn't even here!"

"Perhaps not. But whatever sick scenario plays out tonight, there's evidence all over the place linking him to it. It's *his* castle." Lizzie's already stronger, the effects of the gas fading quickly. She puts her face close to Iris. "His plan is to torture you ... us. We just have to collect the evidence."

"How?" Aanay's voice is hopeful. "What's your plan? How are you going to *take down Gold*?"

Lizzie looks at her brooch then glances at Ben and he nods. "We're recording," she says eventually. "Everything that happens, we're recording it."

"*He's* recording." Iris points at the camera on the ceiling. "So what?"

"So, when this is over ... we'll go to the press." Lizzie's hesitation suggests to me that it isn't the press she's thinking of. What's her *real* plan?

"Gold owns the press." Iris turns from Lizzie as if she's bored of her. I can't tell how much of what Iris does is an act and how much is real. "Even if you get out of here, your 'story' will come to nothing."

"Maybe, maybe not." Lizzie folds her arms.

"I'll help." Aanay almost trips over his feet in his rush to Lizzie's side. "Whatever I can do, I will."

He looks at Lizzie intensely. "He has to be stopped."

Bella relaxes her hold on Dawson's wound and his blood pumps over her knuckles. "Don't be ridiculous, Aanay." She tosses her head and looks up at him. "When we get out of this we will be *promoted*. It's what we all want, isn't it? We'll be running our own companies. We'll be rich. Your parents will be proud."

Aanay snorts. "My parents don't even understand why I'm *interning* for Gold. They'll never understand it if I start running a company for him. They don't care about material things. They only care about living a good life."

"Well, *I* want to run my own company," Bella snaps. "My father will be proud. After what happened with stupid Matteo … and then the professor…" She shakes her head. "I won't let you take down Gold. I have my own dream."

"Gold's killed me." Dawson's voice is barely a whisper, but we all fall silent to stare at him. "And before I die, I want to know he's payin'. Dad'll carve him up if he finds out what happened to me." His eyes bore into Ben's. "*Screw* the press. Get that recording to Ian King — you understand me? He's always got a man in the King's Head in Lambeth. You can find him that way."

"Ian King," Ben repeats and he looks at Lizzie, their expressions inscrutable.

"You aren't going to die, Dawson," Bella laughs. "Grady is going to sew you up, good as new. Then you'll want that company to run, won't you? Why kill the goose that lays the golden egg?"

Aanay clenches his fists then quickly uncurls them. More and more I'm thinking that Aanay actually *is* what he seems. No one could be that good an actor. No one except me.

"Bella," he murmurs. "You saw what happened to Dawson. You saw the g-gas in the pantry. What makes you think you'll get out of here alive? You can't run a company if you're dead."

"I am getting out of here," Bella snaps. "I'm not stupid. I will solve his puzzles, I will get out of the castle and I *will* get a promotion." She looks at Iris. "What about you? Are you with me?"

Iris nods. "I don't want the company I work for to be damaged. It's a good job. Anyway, I don't believe it's possible, even if I did want to. He's watching now." She points at the camera. "He knows exactly who is for and against him." She tries to snatch Lizzie's brooch but Lizzie leaps backwards, putting the butcher's block between them.

"A good job?" Lizzie is incredulous. "Seriously? How many businesses put you in danger like this?"

I glance at the clock and exhale. Fifteen minutes have already ticked by. "We don't have time for this." I gesture with the needle driver. "In forty-five minutes, this room will be filled with gas, or something worse will happen. Listen, except for Bella, Gold has recordings of all of us, right? Videos he's threatening to release if we don't do as he wants?"

Iris nods slowly.

"So, at least for now, think of this as a way to turn the tables. To have a recording on *him*. We don't have to decide what to do with Lizzie's evidence right away."

Ben nods. "Iris, isn't it?" He smiles at her acknowledgement of him. "Let us take our recording, and if you get out of here, you'll have a way to get what *you* want out of Marcus Gold for as long as you want."

"Leverage," Bella muses. "I don't hate that idea.

Gold wants a recording so he can compromise me, but instead I would have something to hold over him."

"For you, it's leverage," Lizzie says, keeping the block between herself and Iris. "For us, it's evidence."

Ben looks at her. "Lizzie," he says gently. "The important thing is they're letting us take the recording. We can decide what it's going to be used for later."

"He's right." I add my voice to Ben's. "We can't spend any more time arguing. *I* have to put stitches in Dawson. You've got to find the way out of this room." Stabbing the curved end of the needle into Dawson's skin, I prod it through. Dawson grunts as I find the emerging end and tug the needle up so that the thread slithers through his skin. Then I tie a double knot and snip the thread with the small scissors Ben had in the kit.

"One down, about twenty to go." I look at Dawson's face. "This isn't going to be neat."

"Do I … look like I … care?" Dawson bites out the words.

Already my hands are covered in blood and I'm finding it hard to see where to put the needle next.

I use Bella's fingers as a guide, poking the metal into Dawson's stomach just in front of her fingertips. I wipe my forehead and look up at the clock again. "Why isn't anyone moving? Aanay?"

He nods, trying not to look as I make the next stitch.

"You're good at this." Bella's watching me closely.

"His dad's a doctor," Ben mutters as I make the third stitch.

"He expected me to know certain things." I feel a gaze and look up. The camera is focused on me, its lens narrowed on my fingers, like an interested eye. I make another stitch.

Lizzie slaps the butcher's block, as if to wake herself from a dream. "I'm going to look around."

Immediately Ben looks at her. "Be careful."

"I'll check under the sink – see if there's a reason the taps aren't working." She weaves her way to the sink and, despite the job I'm doing, I watch her open the cupboard. "This can't be right." She looks up. "The taps aren't attached to the pipework, it's like they've broken apart."

"How?" Ben can't move. He's holding Dawson for me, but Aanay stands beside Lizzie.

"She's right. When the doors locked, the taps must have automatically dismantled. This'll have something to do with the solution in here. Should I reattach them?"

I think for a moment, but Bella answers. "Not yet." She looks at Dawson. "What if it sets off a trap. Maybe you should look around some more first?"

Aanay backs gratefully away from the kitchen sink and Lizzie straightens. "I'm going to let the washing-up water out at least. It stinks." She dunks her hand in the sink and pulls the plug. The water gurgles away and when she steps back, I let out a breath I hadn't even realized I was holding. I catch Iris's eye. She too had been watching Lizzie as if waiting for her hand to drop off.

"There're cookbooks over there." Ben tilts his head towards a shelf on the wall next to the range oven. "In the pantry the answer was in a recipe: Golden-syrup dumplings."

Lizzie races to the shelf and starts to pull down books.

"Then it probably won't be in here," Aanay says. "The rooms shouldn't repeat. If the answer was in a cookbook in the pantry, it won't be the same anywhere else."

Lizzie stops. "Well, what *should* I look at next? Should I open those cupboards?"

I make another stitch as the camera blinks down on me.

Lizzie glowers at Iris. "Aren't you going to help?"

Iris folds her arms. "I'm fine observing. I'll let you know if I think of something you should be doing."

Lizzie's glare could cut glass and I snigger as I make the next stitch. The wound is halfway closed now, but Dawson's skin is so pale, he's transparent. He's lost far too much blood. To be honest, I suspect this is an exercise in futility. I look at Ben as I tie the next knot. He's still watching Lizzie, a tic moving in the corner of his eye. He isn't looking at me. It's as if he can't. Does holding the bleeding Dawson remind him of Carmen's death? It would be odd if it didn't, I suppose.

I say nothing, instead I check the position of Bella's fingers and jam the needle into Dawson's flesh once more.

"I'll help you open the cupboards, Lizzie." Aanay starts forwards. "If there's one that doesn't want to open, don't force it."

Lizzie nods and again I look up, watching as Aanay starts opening wooden doors one after the other. The cupboards contain the things you'd expect in a large kitchen: one has gadgets in, another has pots and pans, another cups and plates. There's a drawer of cutlery, another of utensils.

"It all seems really ... normal," Lizzie mutters and she looks at the clock. "Should we look at the taps again?"

"Not yet." I gesture with my chin. "What about the oven and the fridge?"

There's a large American-style fridge-freezer by the door we entered through. Lizzie opens it and looks inside. "Just food." She starts to move the packets, looking under them, appearing disappointed when she doesn't find whatever it is that she expects. "Nothing."

She goes to the oven and tries the door. She pulls harder.

"*Stop!*" I have to shout it and she leaps backwards, exhaling with sudden terror as she realizes what she almost did.

"It's stuck," she whispers and Aanay touches her shoulder.

"It has to be part of the solution."

Ben looks at Lizzie. "We could try and take it off the hinges. I've got tools in my bag."

Aanay shakes his head. "That's not how escape rooms work. We'll be able to open it easily once we work out the puzzle."

The clock is saying that half our time is already gone. I put the final two stitches in Dawson's wound and lean back on my heels. Bella stands up with a moan of relief. But then she looks at the sink. "How am I meant to wash my hands?" She raises her bloody fingers with a scowl. "Also, I need a drink and my bottle is empty." She glares at Dawson, who forces a small smile.

"Thank you … for helping me … Bells."

"Just don't die and make it a waste of time." She heads to the wine rack. "Maybe there'll be something decent in here."

Dawson catches my eye. "Good job … mate." His teeth are still gritted against the pain.

I shrug and look at my work. The stitches are black against his white stomach, the gash now clenched like a piece of chewed rawhide, blood seeping between the stitches. They're too widely spaced really. I pick up the bandages and Ben lifts Dawson's shoulders as I wrap them around him, tying a knot at his waist. Then I wipe my hands on my trousers and Ben lays Dawson back down.

"Sorry, man, I've got to help Lizzie." Ben gets up, repacks the medical kit and slides it back into his bag.

Dawson nods tiredly, letting his head fall back on to the flagstones.

I stand with him and check the clock. "We've got to get moving." The timer is still ticking away, another five minutes gone.

Iris is leaning against the butcher's block. I don't expect much help there.

Lizzie stands by the freezer, her fingers fiddling unconsciously with her hair. "Does this seem odd to anyone else?" She points at the fridge-freezer and both Ben and I move to her side.

"What?" Ben leans in.

There's a digital display on the front of the fridge, showing the temperature inside. The fridge is set at three degrees. The freezer seems to be set at minus eighty.

Taking a breath, I open the freezer. It's empty.

I close it again. Minus eighty flashes and then settles into a steady glow.

Ben frowns. "That can't be right."

"This is good!" Aanay is at my shoulder, I hadn't even heard him move. "Numbers are often important in escape rooms. Are there any others?"

"I'll look over here." Bella starts pulling wines from the rack. "Some of these are *terrible*." She's creating a circle of bottles around her feet. "I thought Gold would have a really good wine cellar."

"This is the kitchen. Maybe it's all cooking wine?" Lizzie raises an eyebrow.

"Golden-syrup dumplings!" Aanay shouts. I turn to stare at him. "In the pantry – they said the solution was golden-syrup dumplings."

Ben nods. "So?"

"In the dining room, the straws we needed to put in the wall—"

"Were gold," Bella finishes.

"Gold *coloured* anyway." Iris shrugs.

"I think maybe, *gold* might be a clue in more than one room, like a theme," Aanay says.

I watch Lizzie look around, a frown slicing a vertical line between her eyes. "But there's nothing gold in here."

"Look for something, *anything*!" Aanay orders.

"Well, it's not Italian, but at least there's *one* decent bottle," Bella calls, pulling a final bottle from the rack. "Now I need a corkscrew." She looks at the label triumphantly and then pauses. She laughs. "This bottle is from Cedar Creek in Australia."

Aanay folds his arms. "I don't think you should drink it, Bella. You need your mind sharp."

"Cedar Creek?" Bella looks at us as if we're stupid. "It's on the *Gold* Coast."

Aanay claps his hands. "Well done! Are there any numbers?"

"The last digit of the year has been scratched out." Bella holds up the bottle. "Now it says two hundred."

Lizzie frowns and tugs at her fringe. "That gives us minus eighty and two hundred. What can we use them for?"

Ben goes to the sink. He bends his dark head over the taps. "I think it's time to fix these." He kneels by the cupboard and puts his head inside. "The pipes are colour coded. Red pipe to red connection and blue to blue. I just need to screw this here … and this here." I force myself to relax as I watch him, my fists open by my sides. He stands and reaches for the cold tap. "Ready?"

"What could possibly happen?" Iris says mockingly.

Ben turns the tap and water trickles out. "That's odd." He turns it off and on again. More water squirts into the sink. "It only turns halfway now. It worked fine before."

"Halfway?" Lizzie touches his shoulder and he leans into her. "One hundred and eighty degrees?" She looks at Aanay.

He nods at her. "Could be. Minus eighty, two hundred and one eighty."

Bella pushes Ben to one side. "At least now I can wash Dawson off my hands."

Ben steps out of her way, taking Lizzie and Aanay with him. Bella turns the hot tap. Instead of water trickling from the spout, as it did with the cold, there's a hiss and water squirts upwards, from the centre of the handle. It hits Bella in the face.

Her hands slap over her cheek and she starts to scream wildly. "It burns, *merda*, it burns!"

Immediately Lizzie is at her side, trying to pull her

hands from her face. I stare at the tap. Where the water is hitting the work surface, it's spitting, pitting the thick wood and leaving yawning blisters in the varnish. The smell of burning wood mingles with the scent of Dawson's blood and a new odour: that of burning skin and hair. It isn't water coming from the tap. It's acid.

"Lizzie, don't touch her face!" I leap across the room and pull Lizzie away from the screaming Bella. Dawson is levering himself up, shouting, demanding to know what is happening. Aanay is standing with his own face half covered, watching through widened eyes.

"Stay away from the tap, Ben!" I shout as he starts forward to turn it off. "Don't let it touch you."

"What—?" Ben sees the work surface for himself and stops. His eyes go to Bella and he gasps.

"We need water." I look around wildly.

Lizzie yanks her arm from my grasp and runs to the fridge. "There're bottles in here."

She throws them to Ben, and I grab Bella by the arms. "Let me see your face." She's still screaming, shaking her head wildly. "Move your hands!"

She shakes her head again.

"Ben!" I shout.

But it's Iris who comes over. She grips Bella's wrists and yanks them down, hard. Bella screams again and I catch a glimpse of her. Acid has burned the skin of her right cheek and temple. Her eyebrow is half gone, and I can see patches of skull through the blood and sinew revealed by the shrivelled skin. Against all the odds, it missed her eyes: she won't be blind.

Iris swears and I grip Bella's head and hold her immobile. Iris still has hold of her wrists. Bella's mouth is open, but her screams have turned breathless. Her eyes roll wildly in her head. I wonder if she's going to pass out.

"Ben!" I shout, but he's already moving. He empties the first water bottle over Bella's face. Her skin bubbles. She sobs. He starts on the second bottle.

I glance up in time to see Aanay. He has a ladle in one hand and is standing as far from the sink as he can, while prodding at the tap with the metal handle.

A moment later and the acid has turned off, and a cruel hissing I hadn't realized I'd been hearing

141

vanishes from the edge of sound.

For a heartbeat we're all silent, panting, and then Bella's sobs reverberate round the room.

"Somebody, help her!" Dawson gasps.

"To the sink." I push her forwards but Bella bucks against me, terrified. "The cold tap's working," I remind her. "We have to get your face under running water!"

"I no longer have a face." Bella is screaming again. "You think I don't know!" Her knees collapse. I glance at Iris. She rolls her eyes but eventually helps me carry Bella towards the sink, while Ben turns on the cold tap. I lean over the bowl, pushing Bella with my body until she's forced to bend. Iris grips the undamaged side of her face, holding her under the water. I release her and stand back. Her white blouse is spattered with blood and her face ... I tear my gaze from her injuries and blink. There on the tiled splashback, where the acid has sprinkled, the ceramic has burned off. Underneath is a number: 120.

Chapter Twelve

Grady

"I have to send in our report."

I'm meant to be doing homework but when Mrs Harper appeared on the doorstep, I stopped so I could listen. Father doesn't know I spent a whole day this Easter creating a hidden vent between his study and my bedroom. I've been waiting for them to get together in there for a while.

I know she and Father have a secret, but what? They aren't having an affair. If I thought I was about to hear Will's mother getting freaky with my widowed father, I'd be racing for the door. I thought maybe it was something to do with the fact he was being sued by that old lady, but I haven't been able to find any connection. What's their secret?

"You've got a couple of days yet." Father's voice is cold. Definitely not an affair.

"I need your data today. And the recordings of the boy's time in your den last week." Mrs Harper is speaking, her tone clipped. "I have other things to be doing."

Recording of our time in the den? I glance towards the

stairs that lead to the basement, my 'den'. I'd been in there with Ben and Will last week. Just chilling, as Ben called it. Father recorded us. How? Why?

"I haven't finished going through it." My father sounds irritated.

"It isn't up to you to do that. He's paying us extra for recordings of their interactions, not an analysis of them."

"It's fascinating." My father again. "You know, of course, that you failed with Ben?"

Will's mother is silent for a long moment and I can imagine Father watching her, gauging her reaction. "In one *way*," she says eventually. "But his relationship with Will remains intriguing. This month's data, please. And the recording?"

There are long beats of quiet as Father presumably finds what he needs and passes it over.

"You think you have some sort of special relationship with him, but you're going to have to fall in line when he decides what to do with our sons."

"He won't do anything to hurt them. He needs them."

"Both of them? All of them?"

"Shut up, Theo."

I listen to her leave and realize that my heart is thumping. Who is 'he' and what is going on?

▼

"Grady, are you listening?" Iris snaps at me. "How long do we keep Bella under the tap?"

The clock is ticking silently. Twenty minutes left. I nod towards it. "Just keep her there as long as you can." I pinch the bridge of my nose. "All right, we've got twenty minutes left—"

"Nineteen now," Ben corrects me.

"Nineteen." I lick my lips. "And we've got some numbers, right, Aanay?" Aanay is still shaking, his eyes flicking between Bella and Dawson as if he's stuck in a loop. "Come on, Aanay – speak to me."

Aanay doesn't take his gaze from Bella. She's bent over the sink, her legs like a foal's. She's gripping the sink edge and screeching as Iris holds her down by the back of her neck. The sound of trickling water mingles with her gulping sobs. The noise is making it hard for me to think.

"What can we use the numbers for?" Lizzie calls over Bella's shrieks, her hands clenching and unclenching as if she wants to help but doesn't know how. "There's nowhere to enter them.

145

It's not like it was in the pantry, there's no keypad. The door needs a *real* key."

"There's only one place." Ben is moving towards the oven as he speaks. "We have to get into the oven, right?"

Aanay gives a tight nod.

"Well, the oven has a dial with numbers on it. It goes up to two sixty."

"Yes!" Lizzie cries. "It's like a safe."

Ben tilts his head. "That's what he thought."

"He?" Lizzie frowns.

"Me." Ben laughs oddly. "I meant that's what I thought. I'm stressed, OK?"

"OK." Lizzie's expression is tight as she watches him. There's something going on there. Something I should know about.

Ben kneels by the oven and Lizzie grips his shoulder. "Be careful."

He gives her hand a squeeze, but his attention is on the dial. "What were the numbers again?" He touches the knob. "One eighty, eighty…?"

"Two hundred, one twenty," Aanay whispers.

Ben mumbles to himself. I can't hear what he's saying, but Lizzie stiffens. Then he looks at Aanay.

"Which should I try first? If it's like the pantry, they have to be in the right order."

"There's nothing to indicate any order anywhere." I look around the room as if a list will present itself. "Maybe … numerical?"

"Numerical?" Ben looks at Aanay, who shrugs.

"OK then." He turns the knob to the right. "Eighty." We all freeze. There is only the sound of Bella's crying and the running tap. Dawson groans as he lifts his head, trying to see. A long minute ticks by and nothing changes. Ben looks up. "I felt something, a click."

"All right." I lean forwards. "One twenty next." I can feel the camera on our backs, see the clock ticking on the wall above us. Twelve minutes left. I swallow as Ben turns the knob.

"Another click," he says. "Now one eighty."

"Are we sure that one eighty is one of the numbers?" Lizzie says with a frown. "It wasn't written down, not like the others. It's just … a guess. What happens if we put it in and it's *wrong*?"

Ben ducks his head, muttering under his breath. Lizzie digs her nails into his shoulder, but he ignores her. I move closer, listening.

"What do you think? Do I go to one eighty or two hundred? It takes a moment for the click to happen, I can't just blow past it and see how it feels! So, pick one. But what if it's wrong? It'll hurt us."

"Ben," Lizzie whispers.

"What's wrong with him?" Iris demands from the sink.

"Nothing!" Lizzie snaps. "We just don't know which number to go to. If we're wrong…"

"I'm going to one eighty," Ben snaps. He turns the dial, there's a slight pause then he swears, yanks his hand back and sticks his fingers into his mouth. The dial is glowing red.

"Wrong number." I crouch to look at the dial. "It burned you?"

Ben nods. Lizzie is already getting cream out of their medical kit and handing it to him.

I tilt my head as I examine the dial more closely. "It's not cooling."

"We can't touch it like that," Iris says from behind my back. She has abandoned Bella, who's kneeling beside the sink with her face in her hands. I'm curious to scope out her injuries. More interested to see how she'll take the loss of her beauty.

"Tea towels." Aanay is standing next to an open drawer. "Wrap your hand before you touch the dial." He hands one to Ben.

"Maybe someone else should take over." Lizzie turns and looks at Iris. "How about *you*?"

"I don't think so." Iris retreats and folds her arms.

"Why not? Why should *Ben* take all the risk? This is *your* corporate-bonding whatever. Not ours. *You're* meant to be doing this stuff, not us." Lizzie's eyes are blazing.

"You broke in here – so you take the risks, same as us!" Iris snaps.

"But it isn't the same as *you*, is it?" Lizzie takes a step nearer to her. "You haven't done anything. So, now it's *your* turn." She snatches the towel from Ben and throws it at Iris. "Wrap up."

Iris lets the towel fall to the floor and makes no move to pick it up. "Why should I?"

"Why should *we*?" Lizzie counters.

I look at the clock. We have five minutes left. "That can't be right! There were twelve minutes on that before."

The others all turn to look.

"It did the same in the pantry," Lizzie whispers

149

hoarsely. "When we got a number wrong, it made the clock jump."

"Well, *someone* has to move the dial!" I let myself yell. It feels good. "And someone else soak another tea towel for Bella's face, I can't *think* with all her noise." I pick the towel up from the floor by Iris's feet and clench it in my fist. Aanay's right, if I wrap my hand, I should be able to touch the dial. It represents a risk, but a small one. And when the next crisis comes up, I can say it's someone else's turn.

"Are you sure, Grady?" Lizzie murmurs, but I just shove her out of the way. Ben is still kneeling by the oven, muttering to himself, holding his hand to his chest.

"Two hundred, right?" I put my hand to the dial. It's still blazing-hot and the tea towel immediately chars. My hand warms but I'm not burning yet. I turn the dial. As Ben said, there's a click when I put it to two hundred. Then the oven door springs open. I release the dial and peer into the oven. "There's a key." I reach in awkwardly with my wrapped hand and lift it out.

"Is it for the main door?" Iris asks.

I stride towards it, shedding the tea towel as I go.

We have three minutes left. I put the key into the lock, take a breath and turn. "It works."

"We can get into the gallery!" Iris actually smiles. "The entrance hall is right there."

Aanay kneels beside Bella and takes her hands. He pulls them from her face. I try to see, but his body is in the way. I see his shoulders stiffen, then he presses the dripping towel to her cheek. Wet hair is plastered to the other side of her face.

Ben picks up his pack and helps a groaning Dawson to his feet. Aanay lifts Bella, letting her lean on him as he guides her across the room.

"We did it." Ben gives the finger to the camera in the centre of the room. "Let's get out of here."

Lizzie catches my arm as the others file past. "What is it?" I look at her.

"Grady." Lizzie points to the butcher's block in the centre of the kitchen. A set of knives is sitting in the centre, blades gleaming from a notched wooden slab. There's an empty slot on the left side of the block. "That was full when I sat there before … there's a knife missing."

▼

The windows in the gallery are barred, just like the ones in the kitchen and dining room. I can still see through them: the fountain in the forecourt is glittering in the moonlight, the roses colourless in the dark. They let in a little light; enough to illuminate the paintings on the walls opposite, but not enough to alleviate the depth of the shadows between them.

As we enter the gallery, I expect lights to come on as they did when we went from the kitchen to the dining room, but nothing changes. The corridor remains shrouded in gloom.

All the doors along the gallery are closed, and there are keypads beside each one.

One of the psychopaths among us has a knife now.

My brain keeps going back to that. We were all distracted in the kitchen at one time or another. The most likely person to have it is Iris, but Aanay could have picked it up too. He says he'd never touch a weapon again, but realistically he could be as far along the spectrum as any of us and cleverer. Or was Bella less hurt than I'd thought, pretending her injury was debilitating so she could go and snatch the weapon when everyone was looking at the oven?

"I'm getting out of here." Bella runs for the door that leads to the forecourt, one hand pressing the towel to her face. Where would she hide a knife?

Aanay's loose suit has more places to conceal a weapon. I pinch the bridge of my nose. Why hadn't *I* thought to take a knife? I hadn't even noticed them, too busy playing doctor.

Bella is hammering at the door now, demanding to be let out. "I need help, Gold," she is yelling. "Be reasonable, we got this far."

"It won't work, Bells," Dawson grunts. He's still leaning on Ben.

He's the only one I'm sure isn't armed. He never left the floor. But … what if someone *passed* him the knife? I shake my head. The one thing I'm certain of is that the only people who would be willing to team up with anyone else, at the moment, are Ben and Lizzie, and they never even met Dawson before.

"What about the other door?" Aanay gestures. The main entrance is further down the gallery.

"I'll look." Lizzie runs through the gloom, past the painted gazes of milkmaids and serving girls, children in a classroom and a fat-faced publican, until she reaches the steps. She takes them two at a time and looks at the door. She doesn't even try to open it. She turns and calls back, "It's barred."

Bella sags against her own door with a moan.

"Do we really have to go into another room?" Ben looks at me. "There has to be a better way."

"This is a plan of the castle!" Lizzie is walking back from the front door, but she stops in front of the castle plan, next to the Caravaggio. It's lit by an outside lamp, which is now casting its glow through the window and directly on to the image.

"What other rooms are there?" Ben asks.

Her lips move as she reads them to herself. Then she points. "The armoury's that way."

"Sounds … dangerous," Dawson croaks and the fingers of one hand flutter over his bandages, the other is gripping the book in his trouser pocket.

Lizzie looks at the map again. She points the other way down the corridor. "Laundry, servants' quarters, two guest bedrooms, lift, staircase. We could try another floor?"

"I'm not going downstairs," Iris says. "I looked at that map earlier. There's a dungeon down there.

That's got to be worse than any armoury!"

"What's upstairs?" I look at the open staircase further along the corridor.

"Chapel, playroom, master bedroom, study, classroom, a couple of children's rooms, a widow's walk," she reads.

"That's right." Aanay raises his head. "The butler said Gold raised his children here."

"What's a … widow's … walk?" Dawson frowns. He's shaking so severely now that I'd be worried, if I cared. Carefully Ben helps him sit, leaning him against the wall in the shadows between windows.

Iris answers him. "It's a walkway along the outside of a tower."

Lizzie gazes at Ben with wide eyes. "Outside?"

He strides to her side and catches her arm. I follow him. They're standing under a dreadful still life of fruit in a bowl. There's something going on with those two, and if it's going to be a problem I need to know.

I reach them in time to hear them urgently whisper.

"We've got rope." Ben is gripping her. "We can climb down from the widow's walk, run to the

155

beach, get help for Bella and Dawson."

Lizzie swallows. "I want to, Ben. I really do. It's just..." She looks down at her camera-brooch.

"You don't think you've got enough evidence recorded to nail Gold." I step nearer as I fill in the rest of her sentence for Ben's benefit. He glances at me and there's a flash of something in his eyes. He doesn't want me joining in this conversation.

Tough.

"We've got what happened in the pantry," Lizzie says. "But he could argue that we weren't meant to be there, that we'd been contained for our own good, that we wouldn't have been hurt by the gas if we hadn't started messing with the keypad."

"What about the kitchen?" Ben points out. "What about Dawson and Bella?"

"We haven't got a recording of what happened to Dawson." Lizzie sighs. "We've only got what happened to Bella. And ... I'm worried he'll say that if you hadn't messed with the taps..."

Ben shuts his eyes. "That's true."

I lean closer to Lizzie. "You're saying there's a chance you can get out now, but you don't want to go yet?"

She bites her lip and looks at Ben. He still has his eyes closed. "We came here to nail Gold," he mutters. "But what about Lizzie? It's all too dangerous. Acid coming out of the taps, blades coming out of the walls. It'll be for nothing if we don't nail Gold. But what if she gets hurt. *We could get killed in here.*"

I meet Lizzie's eyes. "Is he all right?"

"Yes." Lizzie touches his face. "Ben?" He blinks at her and she strokes his cheek. "What do you want to do?"

He turns from her to look at the map. "What if I go upstairs and scope it out? We might not even be able to get to the walkway."

Iris stamps towards us with a sneer. "Whatever you three are planning, you might want to know that none of these doors will open."

I turn to see Aanay trying the kitchen door. The key we just used isn't working any more.

"I think the lock only turns from the inside." Aanay drops the key on the parquet floor. "We need a code to get into each room."

"So, what do we do?" Bella is still slumped against the door. "Stay in the corridor until someone comes to let us out?"

Lizzie jerks her face towards me; her face is drawn. She's got a problem. If we wait in the corridor all night, there'll be nothing to record and no way to take down Gold. If we go into another room, then someone else could be badly hurt, or worse. It's a decision she can't make. *I* don't have that problem. *I* have no conscience.

"They might never come to let us out." I look pointedly at Dawson. "*He* won't make it without a hospital, and you need one too, Bella. Your face will get infected and without antibiotics you could ... well. We can't wait forever." I turn to Ben. "You wanted to check out the upstairs. Maybe there's *one* door that opens. Maybe that's the way we're meant to go next."

Lizzie glowers at me. "If Ben goes upstairs, we all do."

Dawson rasps out a laugh. "I ain't climbing stairs ... not if I don't have to." Speaking has hurt him. He clutches his stomach and wheezes.

"I'm not risking it." Bella presses back against the locked portal to the outside world. Her shoulders are hunched, as if she's trying to hide from prying eyes. "What if someone's on their way to open this door and we get stuck up there?"

The cameras on the ceiling whirr as we speak, tracking each of us. The eyes in the paintings, so many of them, seem to follow our every move. I can't help looking at the shadowy image of Abraham painted by Caravaggio. His son is still screaming. He'll be screaming forever.

"There's a lift," Ben says eventually. "We could take the lift up, if Dawson can manage it."

Dawson exhales shakily. "If I have to … go up, I'll take the lift. But … can someone find out if there's even an … open room before I move?"

"I'm not going into another of those rooms." Bella is still pressing the towel to her face. "You can't imagine how much this hurts!" A single tear traces her one perfect cheek, glistening in the faint light.

Lizzie snatches their bag from Ben and rushes towards Bella. "I'm so sorry, I didn't think!" As she walks, she's digging in the pack. She pulls out their medical kit and drops the bag beside Bella so she can hold a couple of cardboard packets to the light. "I can't see – which are the painkillers?"

Ben has followed her. He touches her shoulder. "You deal with this, I'm going upstairs." He takes the medical kit, puts it back into his bag and slings it over his shoulder. "I'll check whether or not we can get to the widow's walk and find out if any of the other doors open. I won't go into any rooms."

"I'll come with you." Lizzie glances at him, before squinting back at the boxes in each hand. "Wait a moment."

But Ben is already walking away.

"Hang *on*, Ben!" Lizzie calls, frustrated. "It's too dark to read this tiny writing. These packets look the same."

Ben takes a couple of stairs and pauses, waiting. A camera follows him, purring as it rotates on its axis, its red light narrowing.

Then there's a metallic clank from the ceiling above him. Lizzie turns with a cry, and plunges towards him, but she's too late.

A portcullis descends like a guillotine and Ben throws himself backwards as it slams on to the second step, blocking both the gallery and the basement and almost taking off his toes.

"*Ben!*" Lizzie is screaming but *she's* in no danger, so I stride past. The gaps between the metal on the portcullis are small. Large enough for their fingers

160

to touch, but no more.

Lizzie is sobbing. "What do we do?" She looks at Ben, then at me. I can't help but be struck by the difference in her. On Aikenhead we'd have been looking to *her* for answers. She's a different person now.

Ben picks up their bag. "It's OK, Lizzie."

"How is it OK?" Tears are streaking her face. It's embarrassing.

"I'll get back to you." Ben peers into the dark stairwell. "There's a lift, isn't there? I just have to go up and call it."

"What if it doesn't work?" Lizzie is pressing her fingers against the bars. He touches her fingertips.

"If it doesn't work…" He closes his eyes, thinking. "There must be another way back downstairs."

"There is," Aanay calls. He's gone to check the castle map. "It's a long way round, but if you go through the chapel, you'll find yourself in the games room. There're stairs from there down to the music room. We can meet you."

"What if those stairs are blocked off too?" Lizzie looks haunted.

"Then he can keep going through the games

room and into the library, that room appears on both the first and second floors of the map."

Ben gives a half-smile. "I'll be fine, Lizzie."

"There was gas in the pantry. Acid came out of the tap in the kitchen. *He knows we're here*, Ben. You won't make it through all those rooms by yourself!" Lizzie is letting panic take over. She'll be no use to me like this.

I see Iris rolling her eyes and resist the temptation to do the same. "Try the lift, Ben," I say. "Check the other doors while you're up there. We'll wait for you here."

"Grady." Aanay's voice is shaking as badly as his hand. "Look!"

I follow his pointing finger. Bright against the far wall, a clock has appeared. The seconds are already ticking down.

Bella swears in Italian and Dawson laughs bitterly. Lizzie has turned almost as pale as Dawson.

I exhale. "All right then." I realize that Ben can't see the clock from the stairs. "We've got a countdown clock here."

Ben closes his eyes and mutters something I can't hear, then he reopens them. They look harder somehow and, in the darkness, more grey than blue.

"We'll wait for you as long as we can." I've taken a step back from him. I make myself stand still. "If you don't return in time, we'll find a way to the music room and meet you there."

Ben only nods. I put a hand on Lizzie, but she flinches me off, fixing her gaze on Ben. "I don't want to be on my own with these people," she whispers.

"I'll be back." Ben turns and starts up the stairs. "Keep recording," is the last thing he says before he vanishes into the gloom.

Chapter Thirteen

Lizzie

He's gone. He can't be on his own. He doesn't do well on his own. Not these days. I think of him muttering in the B&B. It's got worse since he saw Grady again. Grady… I force my hands to relax at my sides. I'm surrounded by Gold's hand-picked psychopaths. And one of them has a knife. But then … so do I. My fingers twitch towards the holster, tight on my right thigh. It's been rubbing my skin into blisters all day, but I don't let myself touch it. As far as the group surrounding me is concerned, I'm prey. I don't want them to know that I have claws too. The big question is, if it comes down to it, will I be able to use them?

I take a deep breath and look at them one by one. I don't have anything to fear from Dawson right now and Aanay seems all right, but I'm not a good judge of character, am I? I mean, all those years and I never knew what Will was, or that Ben's whole life was about making sure that his brother never hurt anyone. I never saw what Grady was either. I thought he was just a conspiracy nut, a little weird but basically a good guy. I snort a laugh. It tastes sour on my tongue.

I've been doing my research since Iron Teen. I know what a psychopath is now. I know they can't empathize, not with me, not with each other. Not one of the people standing around me has a conscience. They'll lie to me without remorse and they won't care if I'm hurt. Perhaps they'll be charming, trying to manipulate me into doing what they want.

At least Grady needs me. He wants Gold taken down. Aanay said he wanted to take down Gold too. But can I trust him?

I almost feel as if I'm safer with the girls. Not because they're girls, but because I know they want to stop me. I'll be careful around them, won't lower my guard. I swallow and turn. Bella is still sitting against the door. She's watching me from the brown eye that isn't covered by her wet towel.

"Painkillers, right?" I look at the packets that I dropped on the floor. Ben has everything else with him. I pick them up.

Grady jolts. "I almost forgot! We have a torch. We found it in the dining room." He puts a hand in his pocket. "It's UV light but it should help you read them."

He passes the torch over to me. It's small and heavy; black metal. I find the switch and click it on. Immediately pale blue light illuminates the pills, just enough that I can work out what to give Bella. The other pack turns out to be sleeping pills. I put them in my pocket and start back towards Bella as the light plays over the painting beside the map. It's hideous but somehow arresting. In the moonlight I can see an old man holding a boy down, about to cut his throat. The boy is screaming, yet it's the old man who captures my attention, his eyes are tortured. He doesn't want to do it, but the boy is a sacrifice.

Then I stop. The light highlights numbers scrawled across the bottom third of the artwork. I frown and turn the light off. The numbers vanish. I turn the torch back on and they reappear. Then I turn the light on to the painting nearest me. It's a still life and, under the blue light, the numbers 1287 are revealed.

"What's that?" Iris comes up behind me, her footsteps silent. I jump and put a little more distance between us. Forgetting Bella's pain relief, I walk from painting to painting, shining the light on each. Number after number appears.

"What are they, do you think?" I look at Aanay. He seems to know the most about the situation.

"They have to be the codes for the door keypads." His eyes brighten. I guess he likes solving puzzles. "Each picture must represent a room, and the code gets us inside."

"What's the code for the staircase?" I turn on him. "We can go after Ben."

"No keypad next to the staircase." Grady drops his chin. "Sorry, Lizzie."

Is he sorry? I frown. Maybe he is, this time, because he needs Ben almost as much as I do.

"How do we know which room the numbers are for?" I stare at the painting I'm now in front of. It's a group of people sitting at a table, eating a feast. The number scrawled on the painting is 4593.

Bella says, "That's the dining room. And where are the painkillers?" I pass Bella the packet, trying not to stare. She is still holding the towel against her face but she's on her feet.

"Bella could be right." Grady smiles at her and I try not to gag. Don't tell me he fancies her? No, he doesn't – he can't do. He's manipulating her, just like he did me and Ben for all that time: gentle Grady, foolish Grady, clumsy Grady. Grady with his conspiracy theories. I'm such a fool.

"I think she is." Aanay is running from painting to painting. "The pictures kind of match the rooms on the castle plan."

"There's one way to be sure." Grady is standing by the dining-room keypad. "We try the number."

"You *can't*!" My eyes widen. "Remember, if you put in a wrong number, we lose time."

"Well, we have to know for sure." Iris is at my shoulder. Again. I hadn't heard her move. Once more, I step away from her.

"Doesn't anyone else think this is a bad idea?" I stare around at them, but they're all watching Grady and ignoring me. It's as if I don't exist.

Then Grady looks at me. "I'm doing it."

I turn to the clock. Ten minutes have gone. I keep my eyes on it as the beeping of the keypad sounds behind me.

Then there's the sound of a door opening. The clock ticks on, steadily. Eleven minutes.

"It worked," Grady exhales.

"Then we're right." Aanay smiles. "The pictures represent rooms. Look —" he points — "there's a milkmaid with a cow here and there's a dairy downstairs."

"Yes, there is." Grady has moved to the castle plan and now he's looking at it. "What about the laundry, Lizzie, can you see a corresponding picture?"

Gritting my teeth, I race along the gallery. Each picture is illuminated by a window. "There *is* one here of a woman hanging out clothes."

"And the kitchen?"

"I've found a cooking scene," Aanay calls.

"We need some way to write this all down." I rub my aching head. "Each room and its corresponding painting and code."

There's a beat and then Dawson groans and shifts. I see that he's trying to pull something from his pocket. "Stop. Let me help you." I kneel at his side and put my hand in. The material crackles under my fingers; dried blood. I shudder as I pull out a hardback notebook.

Dawson grips my wrist. "I want that back."

I nod.

"There's a pencil inside." He leans his head back against the wall and releases me.

I open the book and page through, looking for a blank sheet. It's too dark to read anything, I can just see that the pages are covered in handwriting and doodles. Perhaps it's some kind of diary. More evidence against Gold?

I find a blank page towards the back, and standing under a window I start to scrawl a list of the rooms I remember from the plan. "Is that all of them?" I show Grady the book and he compares the list with the floor plan.

"You missed a couple." He shows me and I add them.

"Now we need to find the right pictures and add the numbers."

We walk along the gallery, shining the torch on the paintings, trying to fit each to a room. A couple we aren't sure of. Is the code on the painting of the child playing with toys meant to be for the playroom, the child's room, or the nursery? What about the still life of the rocking horse, or the baby in the cradle? Which was which?

Most are obvious. Or at least logical. I make a note beside the ones we aren't certain of.

"There are so many rooms." I count the list, my heart sinking. "Do you think we're going to have to go through all of them to get out?"

"I don't know." Grady shakes his head. "Maybe…" He looks at the others. "Perhaps we should split up, cover more ground."

"I don't think … that's a … good idea," Dawson rasps. "What happens when … more of us get hurt?"

"He's right," Iris says. "I'm not going anywhere without Grady. We might not have the medical kit any more, but he knows first aid. I assume Lizzie will want to stay with him too." She rolls her eyes. "Aanay and Bella could take a different route with Dawson…"

"I'm not leaving Grady!" Aanay says firmly.

"And I can hardly carry Dawson." Bella shakes her head. "We'll have to stay together."

It was like hearing some psycho rendition of 'one for all and all for one'.

"All right then." I head for the lift, which is something from a Gothic novel, with ornate wooden doors. There's a call button but it isn't lit. I push it anyway and feel a roughness under my fingers. I look closer to find a picture carved on the button, similar to a cross-section of a snail shell. Nothing happens.

"It isn't working," Iris says. She's been following me along the gallery.

I sneer at her. "I hadn't noticed." I try to pry the doors apart but can't get my fingers between them. For a second, I consider using the blade of my hidden knife, but I'm not ready for that reveal yet, and how would I get the lift working once inside? Reluctantly I step away. There really is no way upstairs without going through the armoury.

I keep on past the lift, carrying Dawson's notebook. On the wall opposite the first guestroom there's a small painting, deep in shadow, hardly visible. It shows a woman in black on a castle rampart. Her hair is blowing wildly in the wind, her posture hunched, face twisted with grief.

"That has to be the widow's walk." I make a note of the number, then I run past Iris, back to the staircase. I grip the portcullis that blocks me from him.

"Ben!" I call as loudly as I can. "Ben!"

There's no answer.

"We've found the codes for the doors!"

No answer.

"Ben, you can get to the widow's walk. You've got the rope. If you can't get back to us, you can get out. Go and fetch help. I'll keep recording."

I wait in silence.

"Ben…?"

Grady's hand descends on to my shoulder. "Maybe he's in the lift?"

I turn towards the far end of the corridor where the lift doors are tightly closed. There is no sound of a mechanism, no sense of movement.

"It doesn't work." I turn on him. "Where is he, Grady? He can't have gone into a room."

"Fifteen minutes left," Aanay murmurs from my other side.

"What do you want to do?" Grady's voice is surprisingly gentle. I have to remember that he isn't my friend. He sounds sympathetic, but he isn't. He literally can't be.

I frown at him. "You're giving me a choice?"

"We can wait here for a few more minutes and

keep calling or we can start looking for a way upstairs."

"Through the armoury." I swallow.

"If he tried one of the keypads and got it wrong, he might be…" Grady's eyes flicker towards Dawson and my own widen.

"We'd have heard if something like that happened … wouldn't we?"

"Not if it was fast," Grady says quietly.

"You mean he could be lying up there in the corridor, hurt … maybe dying."

"I don't know." Grady's face twists, as if he wants to say something else, but he doesn't. "It's up to you."

"Why is it up to her?" Iris snaps. "What if we want to try a different room, the laundry, for example, or a guestroom? The real way out could be through any of them."

I whirl on her. "We have to get to *Ben*."

"*You* want to get to your boyfriend, *we* don't." Iris shrugs.

Dawson groans. "That lad has a … bag of tricks. If he isn't using it any more, we should get our hands … on it."

Bella is still standing by the door. "Dawson's right.

You said he had a rope." She tilts her head at me. "We can use it to escape."

I tear my eyes from her to glower at Iris. "See, we *do* all want to get to Ben!" I turn to face the armoury at the end of the gallery. "So, let's go and find him."

Chapter Fourteen

Ben

I'm on my own.

I climb the stairs, unable to look back at Lizzie, knowing that if I do, I won't be able to leave her. If there *is* a countdown clock down there, she has to find a way out of the gallery, not hang around the stairwell hoping the bars will retract. Each step away from her is torture, but I can try the doors, see if I can call the lift. Of course, if the doors *are* all locked up here, I won't be able to get to the widow's walk *or* the chapel. I'll be trapped, waiting for rescue.

What triggered the portcullis? Was it automatic? Any weight on that second step might have triggered it. Or is someone actually *controlling* the traps in the castle? Perhaps they saw a chance to separate me from Lizzie and took it. But why would they want us apart? Are we too dangerous together, too much of a team? Or is something else going on?

Maybe it isn't Lizzie they separated us from. What if

it was Grady?

The thought comes unbidden, as always, sliding into my consciousness.

I silently answer. *Why?*

Our influence on him. Or perhaps they just wanted to remove the bag from play.

The *bag*, of course. Lizzie and I had been talking about getting out using the rope. Now we can't. They must be listening to every word, even the whispered ones.

The voice is a familiar one, mocking me. He always said I was stupid, now I've got his voice in my head constantly telling me.

I grip the bag tighter and turn the corner. I climb the final few steps and halt at the top, breathing heavily. There's another gallery in front of me, but this time it isn't paintings that are hung on the walls. It's lined with framed articles from newspapers and magazines. The headline opposite me reads: *Andalucian villages lose anti-fracking lawsuit against Gold International. School collapse ruled unrelated.*

Another in my line of sight reads: *Gas line explosion kills 132.*

To the right it's: *Marcus Gold enters list of fifty*

richest people on earth.

The voice in my head starts to laugh.

There's no countdown clock up here. I wonder if that will change the moment I step on to the thick carpet.

From below I hear muffled voices. I resolve not to turn back. I take a breath and enter the upstairs corridor. No clock appears. It seems I have as much time as I need to check the doors.

I start with the study. Each door has a keypad, but if Grady is right, then one of them should open. I try each handle: study, master bedroom, tower. None of them work.

I reach the chapel. *This* is my way back to Lizzie. It *has* to open. I gnaw my thumbnail as I push the handle with my other hand. Nothing happens. The keypad glows beside me, as mocking as the laughter behind my eyes. I could try putting in a number, but as my fingers hover over the keys I hear his voice again.

We haven't even tried the lift yet. Perhaps hold off on suicide for now.

I drop my hand to my side. It might *not* be suicide? *Look up.*

I do. There's a thin line in the stonework above my head.

What do you think comes out of there?

Cursing, I step back quickly. If they want me dead, they could activate the trap at any moment.

They won't. There're rules here.

Now who's being naive?

There's no response. Why would there be? When did I start talking to myself and expecting answers? I rub my temple, my head is pounding. I look at my reflection in the glass of the article opposite me. I see Will's floppy hair, eyes glittering with an edge of madness, sharp nose, narrowed lips.

I turn towards the lift. I pass the stairs and keep my eyes turned upwards as I check the classroom door. It remains locked, the trap unsprung.

Grady's looking well. He's got the money, the job that was meant to be ours.

I catch sight of my reflection in another glass, the person looking back at me doesn't look like me, it looks like *him*. I haven't looked like *me* in months. I refocus, losing his/my reflection and seeing the headline: *Gold International charity opens all-girl schools in South Africa.*

He got the girl too. As in, he killed her.

"We're here to help Grady take down Gold. That's what's important. We get our evidence and we get out of here."

Now I'm talking out loud, talking to myself. That's not good, Lizzie wouldn't like it.

Lizzie isn't here. She's downstairs. With him. He already killed Carmen because it benefited him. What happens if he decides Lizzie needs to die? You know he'll do it.

"I can't do anything about it. I can't get back to her." I can feel hysteria rising in a merciless tide. Why won't any of the doors open? What does Gold expect us to do next?

Gold fertility clinic opens its doors in UK.

I check the nursery, the child's room.

Gold lawyers defeat FBI demands to see inside secret Clarksdale facility.

The tower.

All the doors are closed. I'm trapped.

There's always the lift.

He's right. I walk back to the dark wooden doors. The carving on them is a work of art, something that might appear on an old Bible, I'm sure it's a hell scene.

Because the lift goes down. He's amused.

The button next to the lift is unlit. I press it, and nothing happens.

"Nothing's working up here! How do I get back to Lizzie?"

You're not meant to, idiot.

I've got bolt cutters in the bag, rope. Brass knuckles in my pocket, the medical kit. "Why didn't I pack a crowbar? I knew I should have ... stupid, stupid."

Look at the button.

I do. There's an image indented on there. It looks like a snail shell, kind of.

"What is it?"

I know.

"Tell me."

It represents the Fibonacci sequence. We learned about it last year. You weren't paying much attention.

"What do you think it means?" I pound my forehead with my palm. Why didn't I pay attention? I'm so stu—

At a guess, you have to press the button according to the Fibonacci sequence to operate the lift.

"I don't know it."

So, why don't you let me do it?

181

"Are you serious?"

Step back, Ben. This is too hard for you. What use are you to Lizzie right now? It's me she needs here. Let me take over. I'll solve the puzzles for you, I'm not scared of anything. Just take a step back. Go to sleep. When you wake up, this will all be over.

"I don't…"

I'm the best of us to deal with this. And think – Gold doesn't know I'm here. He's prepared for you, but is he prepared for me?

"I don't…"

We've done it before. You can't handle this. I can. Let me look after you for a change.

My head feels thick. He's right. I'm tired and my headache has intensified. I look at myself reflected between the bars of the window opposite the nursery door. At him. I turn away and lean my forehead against the image of hell. It's cold against my skin. I close my eyes and sigh. This gets easier every time. I step backwards…

Chapter Fifteen

Will

I open my eyes and lift my sticky forehead from the lift door. I stretch, popping my limbs as I reach for the lined ceiling. Ben never stands up *straight*.

I push my hair out of my eyes and look at the lift button. I don't know how long I have, what *do* I know?

I can operate the lift. Gold might not be expecting that, Ben's an idiot after all. Once I've done it, though, he'll assume I'll race back to Lizzie. Maybe I can use that assumption. I have a bag with bolt cutters, rope, knuckle dusters. How funny that Ben thought he was packing this stuff to help *him* in the castle, when really they were for me.

I take a moment to imagine tying Grady to a chair. Pounding his face until it's burger meat, using the bolt cutters on his fingers.

Grady killed Carmen. I had *plans* for Carmen.

Yes. I'll enjoy cutting his fingers off. As much as I enjoy *anything* that is. It was a shame that Ben gave the knife I packed to Lizzie. But luckily I found another one in the kitchen. Step forwards, take the knife, step backwards. Ben has a small blackout, remembers nothing. I grin as I touch the inside pocket of the bag. Yes, I'll stab Grady the way he stabbed Carmen, watch him bleed. And then … I'll go for Gold.

"Ben!" The faint reverberation of his name bounces from the stairwell. It almost wakes him and I can't have that.

I press the lift button once then pause. My fingers ache and I look at them. They're burnt. He is *such* a moron! Ignoring the discomfort, I press once again, pause, then twice, then three times.

Lizzie is still shouting, something about codes. Ben squirms at the sound of her voice, presses forward.

Screw. Her.

Five times. Pause. Eight times. The button lights up. Finally! I had started to think that maybe I'd been wrong. The lift doors slide open and I step inside.

What's happening?
I've got this, Ben. Don't worry, go back to sleep.
He does.

Chapter Sixteen

Grady

Lizzie opens the door to the armoury in the end. I stand behind her, with Dawson's weight on my shoulder and his groans echoing in my ear. The suits of armour I had seen before are awaiting us, their empty helmets ominous in the gloom.

"Are you sure about this?" Aanay rasps.

Lizzie doesn't answer, she simply steps forward with the notebook in her hand and we follow, like good little psychopaths. As soon as the door closes, the lights blink on. The now-familiar clock appears above the music-room door and a camera starts whirring. Lizzie holds two fingers up to it. It's childish, but I understand the impulse.

I look for somewhere to lay Dawson, and in the end decide on the centre of the floor, coloured by moonlight shining through the stained glass.

Bella looks at me. "I'll sit with him." Her voice is muffled by the towel she's holding, and it is obviously painful for her to speak. She lowers herself to the floor. The colours from the window stain her blouse like blood.

"I'll let you know if we need you," Lizzie says coldly, without looking at her.

Bella's eyes flash. Lizzie had better be more careful. This isn't the sixth-form common room and, even though she's hurting, Bella is a lot more dangerous than Lizzie realizes.

I'd walked through the armoury quickly last time. Now I look around more carefully. The windows above me show two different scenes. The furthest from me is a joust. One knight is unseating the other from his horse. The other shows a group of three knights surrounding a boat. Under it, carved into the stone with deep slashes, are the words: *She has a lovely face, God in mercy lend her grace.* Immediately I think of Bella and then, surprisingly, of Carmen.

There are five suits of armour spaced evenly along the walls. The scabbards are empty, their weapons are hung on hooks at eye-level: three swords and two spears.

"Now what?" Lizzie looks at us. "These puzzles

were set up for you guys, so what's the solution in here?"

There's a long beat of silence. Iris opens her mouth to snap a response, but Dawson surprises me. "The Lady ... of Shallot," he rasps. He is no longer clutching his stomach. His hands are by his sides as if he doesn't have the strength.

"What do you mean?" Lizzie bends closer to him.

"The ... poem." Dawson's eyes move to the carving under the window, directing us to his meaning. "It's ... Tennyson ... innit."

"*You* know Tennyson?" Iris sneers.

He gathers his strength and sneers back. "You *don't*?"

"How does that help us, though?" Lizzie asks.

Dawson shrugs and closes his eyes.

"There are five knights in the windows," Aanay says, pointing. "And five suits of armour. Two of the knights in the glass have spears, three have swords."

"And?" Lizzie folds her arms.

"At a guess, we have to put the right weapon with the right suit of armour," he says.

"I'm not pulling *anything* off the walls." Iris shakes her head. "Not a chance."

I look around. "Haven't we got something we can use to knock the swords down without touching them?"

"Ben has ... in the bag," Lizzie says mournfully.

"Your boyfriend isn't here, so what *can* we do about this?" Iris stamps towards one of the swords and glares at it, as if she can force it to jump from the wall by willpower alone.

"The only things we have are the torch and notebook." Lizzie sighs and stands below another of the blades. "If one of us stands to the side and pokes it with the end of the torch..."

"Let me look at the walls." I go to Lizzie's side and examine the wall around the sword. "I can't see any gaps or holes. Nothing like there was in the dining room."

"You think it's safe to try and move the sword?" Lizzie's scared. She's right to be.

"*I* think it's safe." Aanay touches her shoulder and she flinches. He drops his hand, looking hurt. "I mean, we have to get each sword down before we can put it with a suit of armour. It'll be then that..." He swallows. "If we put the wrong one in the scabbard..."

"You think *that* will spring the trap." Iris faces him.

Aanay nods.

I take the torch from Lizzie. "Makes sense."

I don't have to do this. I turned the heated oven dial, so I still have that to hold over the others, but this seems like another low-risk action. If I get the swords down, I won't have to put them in the scabbards, it'll be someone else's turn.

"Are you sure?" Lizzie asks, moving away from the wall.

In answer I raise the end of the torch, take a breath and then use it to lever the sword away from its hooks. It comes away easily and clatters to the floor with a clang that reverberates across the room.

I move on to the next sword. It too comes free of the wall, but this time Lizzie catches it by the hilt, then lays it carefully on the floor.

I lift the third free with my bare hands. It's cold in my grip. I resist the urge to swing it and put it down. I pocket the torch.

"Now the spears?" Lizzie is breathless, as if she's been running. I don't know why, it's not as if she's done anything.

The first is splintered at one end, the point crushed. It's not even a weapon any more, just a long stick. It fits perfectly in my hand. I lift it up. It catches on the hook. To move it, I have to twist it. But nothing happens. I take its weight, then lean it against the wall.

The final spear is in good condition, the end sharp. It's weighted differently from the first; heavier at the front. I put it down and look at Aanay. "Which is which?"

He shrugs. "Let's look at the armour, see if there are any clues."

"Sort the spears first," Bella calls. "There're only two of them."

Iris drags her to her feet by her free arm. "You aren't sitting this out."

"I'm *hurt*." Bella is still pressing the towel to her face, fighting to pull away from Iris, but the other girl's grip is relentless.

"So?" Iris curls a lip. "You can still think, walk, talk. *Dawson* can sit this out. You can't. In fact, maybe you should do it all. As you said, you're hurt anyway."

Bella's brown eyes turn to ice and she stills.

With her gaze on Iris, she lets the material fall from her hand and I am unable to look away from the oozing mess that's revealed. The centre of the injury, where the acid splattered against her, is dark grey, like old bone. The skin around the blackened core is oozing red, shiny. Splatter marks reach from the side of her mouth, up her cheek, into one misshapen ear and up past her temple.

She's something from a horror film. One side of her face is perfection, the other eaten away. I can't tear my eyes from her. She's more fascinating to me now than she ever was. It's the contrast. She must be in *agony*.

Behind me, sympathetic Lizzie sobs while Aanay struggles for breath. I ignore them and lean closer to Bella. Iris does the same. As soon as her grip slackens, Bella pulls free and slaps her with a resounding smack.

Iris touches her reddening face. Both girls stand with their shoulders back, clashing eyes full of frost.

The silence is fragmented only by breathing.

Finally Lizzie speaks. "The broken spear should belong to the losing knight. Does one of the suits of armour match the one falling off his horse?"

I tear my gaze from Bella and examine the window, trying to distinguish features on the battling knights.

"He has a squarer helmet," Aanay says eventually.

"What about gold?" Bella sidesteps Iris. "You said gold would be a clue in every room."

"I said it might." Aanay hangs his head.

Dawson exhales noisily, his breath rattling. "The … gemmy bridle glitter'd free … like to some branch of stars … we see." He coughs, his face contorting with pain. "Hung in the *golden* galaxy. The bridle … bells rang merrily … as he rode down from Camelot … and from his blazon'd baldric slung … a mighty silver bugle hung…" He stops.

Iris raises an eyebrow. "And that is?"

Dawson coughs again. "Lancelot … description…"

"Don't talk any more." Lizzie bites her lip as she looks at him. "You're saying that one of these suits of armour is meant to belong to Lancelot. The one with … gems and a bugle?"

Aanay points to the group of knights standing round the boat. "That has to be him, doesn't it?" One of the knights is holding a bugle loosely in one hand. "*He's* Lancelot!"

"And there he is." Bella indicates one of the suits of armour. It's shiny where the others are dull, with a bugle across the front.

"OK, but which is his sword?" Iris gestures towards the three, it could be any of them.

"They're named!" Aanay kneels beside one without touching it. "Look, along the handle – this says *Galahad*."

"What about the other two?" Lizzie lifts the second, turning it to the light. "I've got *Gawain*."

"Then the last one must be Lancelot's." Iris kicks it with a toe, and it clatters towards me. "*You* check."

I hesitate before picking it up. I don't want to look as if I'm obeying her. But I should pick my battles.

"It's not." I squint at the tiny writing. "It says *Dulac*."

"Dulac?" Lizzies comes to my side. "What's Dulac?"

Dawson wheezes a laugh and I turn. "What's funny?"

"It's not … Dulac." Dawson swallows painfully. "It's *Du … Lac*." He clenches his fists as he shifts, trying to get more comfortable, and by the look on his face failing. "Lancelot Du Lac."

"Then that *is* Lancelot's sword!" Lizzie cries.

I tear my eyes from Dawson's. I've seen eyes like that before on the island. He doesn't have long.

"This sword goes into that scabbard." I hand the sword to Iris. "There you go."

Iris shakes her head. "I'm not doing it."

"I turned the oven dial," I am happy to remind her. "I took the swords off the wall. Your turn."

She looks at Lizzie, but Lizzie shakes her head and steps away, keeping her brooch turned towards Iris all the time.

"Aanay can do it." Iris marches over to him. "Here, take it."

Aanay pales and looks at me. "I can't."

Iris grabs his hand, curling it around the sword hilt. "You can. You haven't done much either."

He starts to shake. "You don't understand."

"Yes, I do. Coward! Letting us do the dangerous work."

"I'll do something else. But that's a weapon …
I can't hold it." He yanks his hand back, letting the sword drop. Iris jumps as the blade hits the floor beside her toes.

I sigh. "It's against his beliefs, Iris, you can't

195

make him hold a blade."

"I can do anything I want." Iris looks around the room. "If he isn't going to do it, who is?"

I look at the clock. The minutes are slipping away. I'm still not putting the sword in the scabbard, though, and Aanay never will. That leaves Bella, Iris or Lizzie.

I look at Lizzie. "Lizzie …"

"You want *me* to…" Her face is pale.

"It's the only way out of here … the only way to Ben."

She rubs her eyes, then puts Dawson's notebook in her pocket, steps forward and takes the sword. She lowers her voice, speaking only for my ears. "You suck, Grady." Then she marches over to the suit of armour.

"It goes right there." Iris points.

"Screw you, Iris," Lizzie says and she stands on tiptoe, the hilt of the weapon in both hands, the point towards the floor. Her shoulders are shaking. She hauls in a breath and as she exhales, she slides the sword into the scabbard then leaps backwards.

Nothing happens.

She looks at Aanay. "So, was that right … or?"

196

Aanay spreads his hands. "It must be."

"One down then." Lizzie swallows. "What's next?"

"Galahad and Gawain. What do you know about them, Dawson?" Iris looks at Dawson, then frowns. "Dawson?"

I know what she's seen. Dawson is no longer looking around the room; his head has tipped back, his eyes are closed, his hands are loose at his side.

Bella blinks at him. "Is he...?"

Lizzie runs to his side. "Dawson?" She touches his face. "He's still breathing."

Not for long.

Lizzie takes the notebook out of her pocket. "I said I'd give this back."

"Let me see." I reach over her shoulder and take it. All this time I've been wanting to know what was in the notebook. I flick through and start to laugh.

"What is it?" Bella snatches it from me.

"It's *poetry*," I snigger like a kid. "It's gushy love poetry." I knew it; I knew he wasn't one of us.

Bella is paging through. "*Bella*," she reads. "*If I could run my fingers through her hair, breathe her in like starlight, touch her blossom skin. The music of her—*"

197

"Give me that!" Lizzie snatches the book. "Have some respect." Carefully she tears the page with the codes from the back then she closes Dawson's fingers round the cover. "There you go."

I think I see his hand twitch, maybe I'm wrong. I shake my head. "You're too sentimental, Lizzie."

She ignores me.

I glance sideways at Bella. She's wearing a half-sneer and has arranged her hair so that it covers her like a dark veil.

Lizzie bows her head then rises. "Galahad and Gawain, does *anybody* know *anything*?"

There's a heavy silence.

"One of the suits of armour has a white jacket thing," Aanay says eventually, looking away from Dawson. "The other is green, like the image in the window."

"Yes, but which sword goes with white and which with green?" Lizzie snaps.

I pick up the broken spear. "Let's look at this one again." I stare up at the glowing window. "The helmet is squarer, there's a flower of some sort on his shoulder."

"This one?" Aanay stands beside one of the suits

of armour. "But where do we put the spear?"

"Here for now." I lay the spear next to the armour. "And that means the other spear goes with the last one."

Iris moves it across the floor. "We have to get the swords in the right scabbards," she says. "That's what this is about."

"How do you know?" Lizzie raps.

"I don't," Iris snaps back. "It just makes sense."

"There's no way to know which is which. Not without Dawson." I pick up one of the swords. "Nothing on them except the names." I meet Lizzie's gaze; she knows what I'm going to say. "We're going to have to guess."

"And if we get it wrong?"

"There's a fifty-fifty chance," Iris says.

"You do it then." Lizzie glowers at her and Iris retreats.

"It has to be you, Lizzie." I glance at the clock: half our time has gone. "If you want to get back to Ben."

She walks towards the armour with the green material floating over it. "Green." She says as if there'll be an answer in the colour itself. "Green-

Galahad. Green-Gawain."

"Here, take this one." Iris hands her a sword.

"Which is it?"

"Does it matter?" Iris shrugs.

Lizzie turns the sword over in her hand. "Galahad." Her voice is deeper than usual. I think she might be crying.

She has to stand on her toes again to put the sword in the scabbard. Every eye is on her, the camera above us clicks and whirrs, reminding us of its presence. Her arms are trembling. She poises with the sword in place and then she guides it into place. She lets it go and leaps. Too slow.

There's a click and a whoosh. Lizzie stumbles and gasps out a scream. For a moment I can't see what happened. She's on the floor, her right hand flapping at her left shoulder.

Iris is already striding towards the far wall. I kneel by Lizzie – I still need her. "Let me look."

"Screw you … Grady." She grinds the words out.

I grip her right shoulder. "I have to see."

She shakes her head again, but I roll her. She has no choice but to turn. There's something embedded in her back. Her uniform blouse has a spreading crimson rose on the left shoulder blade.

Aanay drops to his knees beside her and takes her hand. Lizzie gasps a terrified breath. "I ... I can't feel your hand."

"We have to get this out." I touch the metal spoke and immediately my fingers go numb. I swear loudly and snatch my hand back. "It's got something on it. Poison."

"It's OK, I'll do it." Aanay smiles gently at Lizzie. He releases her hand, grips the spike between his thumb and forefinger, grits his teeth and pulls. His fingers slide from the metal, slippery with blood.

"It's not going to work." I stop him as he reaches out to try again and he puts his fingers under his armpit.

"Use the towel." Bella tosses it to us.

I grimace as I catch it, one side is bloody, the other dusty. I find the cleanest corner and wrap it around the spike. Then I pull. Lizzie screams as it emerges. Aanay presses the heel of his hand to the wound and I examine the thing I'm holding. It's about three inches long and wickedly sharp. I lick my lips and slide it into my trouser pocket. Aanay sees me and says nothing.

"It came out of here," Iris says, bending over with her back to us. "There's a hole in the wall under the window."

"If you hadn't been moving…" I look at Lizzie. "If that had hit you an inch to the left, or a bit higher…"

"I get it," she spits. "Aren't I lucky?"

"I can't stitch you up." I tilt my head. "Ben has the medical kit."

"I know." Lizzie drags herself to her feet. Her left arm hangs uselessly at her side. She leans against the wall, tears staining her face. "I–I can't move my left hand, or my arm."

Bella jeers at her. "Tough break."

"Is this going to be permanent?" Lizzie finally looks at me, her expression accusing.

"I don't know, not without knowing what was on the barb."

Lizzie looks at the clock and her lips tremble. "I want Ben." Her voice is very small. She clears her throat. "You'd better swap those swords round."

This time it's Bella who walks to the armour. "Stay right there, Iris," she calls and yanks the sword free.

Iris spins, sees Bella holding the sword above her head and snarls.

Bella strides to the armour with the white tabard and thrusts the sword into place with hardly a pause. Nothing happens.

She points to Iris. "Your turn."

Iris picks up the final sword. Without taking her eyes from Bella, she walks to the last suit of armour. Then she glances at the wall behind her, stiffens her back and drops the sword into place.

The door to the music room hisses open.

Lizzie whispers something to Aanay and he hands her the broken spear. "Thanks." She leans on it as she hobbles towards the exit, her left leg dragging. The numbness must be spreading.

Aanay follows her, and Bella and Iris gather behind him. Dawson lies alone in the centre of the room. The tattooed crown on his arm is spattered with blood. Shafts of moonlight dye his face. The hand round his book has fallen open. He isn't breathing.

I kneel beside him.

It's going to be like the island. The deaths here will be covered up with a clever story. Not a plane crash, this time; maybe a fire, which would have the added benefit of destroying the bodies. If I can get to Ian King with his son's notebook … maybe he'll challenge Gold's version of events, whatever it is.

"Goodbye, Dawson," I murmur. "And don't worry. I'm going to take him down."

Chapter Seventeen

Will

It's a small, two-person lift, with three buttons. There are three floors, so that makes sense. I push the middle button with my thumb and the lift jolts smoothly into movement. It reaches the ground floor and the door slides open. There's no sign of Grady, or anyone else, in the unlit gallery. They've solved the puzzle and gone into one of the other rooms, probably the armoury, assuming Lizzie managed to talk them into heading for the nearest set of stairs.

I don't step out of the lift. Instead I lean against the back wall and let the door slide shut again. I put one hand in my pocket and trace the shape of the knuckle dusters.

I have no way to follow Grady into the armoury. If he and Gold's other pets found the door code, presumably I can find it too, but is there a better way? I want to take Grady by surprise and following him like a puppy isn't the way to do it. Ideally, I'll be waiting for Carmen's murderer in a room he hasn't reached yet. Set my own trap.

I bring the castle plan to mind. Ben only glanced at it earlier in the day, but my memory is better than his. I could wait for Grady on the upper landing, but they're *expecting* to see Ben there, so what good would that do? Ideally, I'd either come at them from behind, which means the library, or I could lie in wait in the chapel. But how do I get into either room?

Deep in thought, I push the topmost lift button again and travel back to the first floor. Then I simply stand in the lift. There's a tiny camera lens above the buttons. I put myself in the middle of the floor, standing as much like Ben as possible, hunching my shoulders. They can't know who I truly am. They can't get suspicious.

The lift really is very small. I frown and turn, letting myself look as Ben-like as possible: *Boo hoo, however will I get back to my girlfriend? I love her so much. Boo hoo!*

The lift is too small. According to the plan, it should be the depth of the ground floor guest bed, but it isn't. It's not even close.

206

I had wondered if someone was controlling the traps. There's no Wi-Fi here, no communicating in or out. If someone *is* controlling things, then they have to be on-site, which must mean there's a surveillance operation in a secret room.

A room that could well be accessed from this lift.

I turn, trying to look as if I don't know what to do, and examine the back wall. It's smooth metal. I look at the side. Then I smile. You'd have to know it was there to see it, but ... I lean closer. There's a seam, nearly invisible; a square panel the size of an iPad on the centre left. I run my fingers carefully around it. There has to be a way to make it open. Experimentally I push and, sure enough, the panel is pressure-activated. It drops open. Inside is a scanner for a key card.

I pinch the bridge of my nose. I don't have a key card, obviously. At least I know I was right, and the door is here. I'll have to use brute force. I feel round the wall until I find what I'm certain is another seam all the way along the edge. The whole side wall of the lift must slide or rise. I open the bag and I'm about to pull out the knife, thinking I might be able to put it into the seam, when, in absolute silence, a crack appears at the bottom of the wall. It widens until there's a gap, and then further. There's only one conclusion I can draw here – they don't know exactly what the contents of my bag are. They don't want the lift door damaged and so they're letting me in.

I straighten, supressing a smirk, and with my hand still inside the bag I palm the knife, sliding it up the inside of my sleeve. Then I wait.

The door opens quickly; it doesn't give me much time to prepare. It's a good thing I'm always ready. It's one of the many things that makes me different from my brother.

The room revealed when it opens reminds me a lot of the one we found under Aikenhead: three of the walls are white and the fourth consists of a bank of monitors, at least one for each room. Under the monitors there's a single piece of laminated paper and a number of switches. These must control the traps. I was expecting something a bit more hi-tech if I'm honest, but then I think about how long this set-up could have been in place, how long Gold might have been testing people in this way.

There's a man on his own in the room. He's sitting

in front of the monitors, facing me. His hair is blond, his eyes grey-blue, his suit crisp, despite the hours he must have been in here. There's a single bottle of water beside the chair.

He stands as I step forwards.

"Good evening, Torben," he says smoothly. "Or may I call you Ben?"

I watch his hands. He doesn't seem to have a weapon, but then neither do I.

"My name is Gold." He's smirking now, expecting a reaction. What would Ben say here? I rack my brains. This is the part I always found hardest: imitating those messy feelings. Usually I didn't bother, unlike Grady. I think he quite enjoys acting, but I prefer to be myself.

I'd gasp.

Ah, he's awake, but he's leaving this to me. Sensible.

I gasp.

"*Christopher* Gold." He expands on his introduction. "I believe you know my father."

Nod.

I nod.

Tell him he doesn't have to do this. He can let you go.

He won't.

I *know that,* you *know that, but it's what he's expecting to hear.*

"You don't have to do this." It's hard to put the emphasis in the right places. Did I sound desperate enough, or did I come across a little bored? I lean into it. "You're not your father. You can let us all go." I think I might have thrown up a little in my mouth.

Gold laughs. I've sold it. And really there is no way for him to know that Ben isn't here. That he's dealing with someone far more dangerous: someone just like him.

I know he'll never let us go, not because he's under the control of his father but because I recognize those eyes. His look a lot like Ben's actually, that same blue. But while Ben's eyes were warm and smiling, Gold's make him look like a wolf: cold, hard, a hunter. He's running the castle because he enjoys it.

"You know," he says conversationally, "it's a shame about Bella. I was hoping she'd get out intact. Now I'll have to spring a trap on her before she finds the way out. It will be a mercy really."

"Wouldn't that be cheating?" I take a step nearer.

He doesn't seem to notice.

He shrugs. "I suppose if it happened to Elizabeth … Lizzie … you'd be there for her forever and ever, face or no face."

Of course *I would.*

"Of *course* I would." This is getting easier. Ben's looking out for me, just like he always did. We're a team.

"You're a fool. I'm not." He glances back at the monitors. "They're in the music room. That's Bella's room. I wasn't expecting the kitchen to get her. If she hadn't tried to help Dawson – and why would she have done that? – she wouldn't have been anywhere *near* the acid tap."

"*Bella's* room?" I take another step nearer.

"Some of the rooms are set up with a particular person in mind – inspired by the individual, if you will. They're meant to have the confidence to *step up* in their own rooms. It makes it more fun. Dawson's room was the armoury. Would you believe he loves poetry? Funnily enough, that's where he died."

React – you should care that Dawson's dead!

"Dawson's gone?" I inject horror into my tone.

"Yes, but that's not the best of it." Gold looks deep

into my eyes. "The trap meant for Dawson got your Lizzie."

What? Ben starts fighting forwards: he wants to go for Gold. My hands twitch, almost under Ben's control again, trying to form fists.

I've got this.

Let me!

You won't follow through. I've *got* this.

He recedes but I can feel him. I can't let him take control again until I've got what *I* want.

What happened to Lizzie? he's screaming. *Is she dead?*

"Is she dead?" Ben's voice blends with mine.

Gold shakes his head regretfully. "She moved at the last moment, and as the toxin didn't get into her spinal cord it should eventually wear off." He smiled. "But she's at a disadvantage going forwards."

"Lizzie's been at a disadvantage before. Didn't you watch the Aikenhead footage? A man like you, I know you did."

"With popcorn." He wets his bottom lip. He'll attack soon.

"Can I see her?" I'm honestly not sure who asked this, was it me or Ben? We both want to.

"Be my guest." Gold gestures towards one of the screens behind him. It's labelled *Music Room*. The picture is crisp and clear, full colour. "Turn the knob in front of you to listen in. I turned it down for our conversation."

I don't turn the knob. I watch them as they spread out through the darkened room, exploring carefully, picking up instruments and putting them down. Bella runs her fingers over the piano keys and moves on. Lizzie is leaning on a long staff.

"Do you want to arm the trap?" Gold asks.

I glance at him.

"Just press that button." He points to a flat square beneath the music-room screen. I want to, I really do, but Ben wouldn't. I glance at the laminated page from the corner of my eye. It's a code list, master codes in case Christopher needs to get into any of the rooms. Interesting.

"I could set them to arm automatically when the doors close, but there's something so satisfying about doing it myself."

"You're sick." I say it without needing Ben's prompting. I'm getting good at this.

Gold reaches across me and presses the button.

In the room the lights go on, the clock appears on the wall. A message appears on the bottom of the screen: *Armed*.

"Just wait till she touches that piano again," Gold says.

"Why are you doing this?" I genuinely want to know. "And how did you know Lizzie and I would be here?"

"Grady *is* clever, I'll give him that. It took us a while, but once he stole those uniforms, we wanted to know why."

"He thought he got away with that, he thought no one was watching…"

"We're always watching." Gold laughed. "His little phone stunt in the toilet – risible."

"Then why didn't you come for us in Wales?"

Gold picks up his water and has a long sip. "I'm bored of explaining. Why do you think?"

I let myself wonder what I would have done in Gold's position and then I nod. "Evidence."

"Go on."

I keep my eyes on the screen as I speak, watching Lizzie lower herself on to a padded chair. Her left side seems to be dead, her arm flops into her lap.

She looks like a useless scarecrow, taken down from its stand and dropped. What *does* Ben see in her?

"You don't know what kind of connections we made in Wales, who might notice we were missing and what story they might tell. We might have set up our own security, secret cameras or something. Whoever you sent for us might have left evidence: blood-spatter, witnesses. Our bodies might have been discovered, or some kind of proof of who we were, that we didn't die in that plane crash. Too many risk factors. Make us come to you, though … we'll likely have closed up our lives in Wales, you don't need to worry about our bodies being found—"

"We have people in Wales as we speak, cleaning out the B&B and removing all evidence of your existence, from the hairs you left in the sink to the sock under your bed. We had a story prepared, but frankly no one has even asked where you went. Now we can have you killed any way we like, with no concerns about repercussions for Gold International."

Do you think he knows about our contact at the NGO? Does he know about Matt?

Ben is worried. I don't answer.

"Why let me in here?" I look at Gold. Any second now...

He smiles again. If I'd been another kind of person, I'd have had ice running down my spine. "Two reasons really." He shifts his stance slightly. "One, you were going to destroy my door. I couldn't have that."

"And the *other* reason?" I already know what it is.

"Well, Ben, I'm bored." Gold spreads his hands.

Yes, that's pretty much what I was expecting.

"And I've never killed a brother before."

There's a kind of a wrench in the back of my mind, where Ben is. Shock and horror. Then he falls silent; he's gone away. He can't cope with Gold's revelation.

I look at Gold's comment from all angles. He's saying that I'm his brother, and he *appears* to believe it. Which means he knows something I don't. There's no question mark over the identity of our mother. Ben remembers her being pregnant. That means Dean Harper isn't our biological father. He's not the kind of man who'd put up with that kind of betrayal, so he doesn't know. I draw these conclusions with lightning speed and squirrel the information away to consider properly later. I'm sure I can use it for something.

Gold expects shock to have frozen me in place. As I'm thinking, he reaches behind his back and then, in one smooth move, thrusts his arm forwards. He's holding a knife.

I grab his wrist in my left hand, halting the knife an inch in front of my stomach and applying pressure. Almost before he realizes what has happened, I take his knuckles in my right hand and *twist*. I turn his hand back towards him, while keeping the tension in my fingers. I feel the moment his wrist snaps. If I wanted to, I could just lean in and jam his knife into his gut, but where's the fun in that?

He shouts and his eyes widen. Ben isn't this quick; he never has been. *I'm* the fighter. I wonder if Gold will work it out, if I should tell him. Would it be satisfying to let him know who I am?

The knife has dropped to the floor. I release him and step away.

Even in his pain he sneers at me. He thinks my move was a fluke, that I let him go because I'm *Ben,* because I'm giving him a chance to stop. Because

I'm weak. He doesn't know I'm just playing. He doesn't know that *I* have a knife too.

He bends and lifts the blade with his left hand; he's holding his other close to his chest.

"Tell me what you meant?" I let more *Ben* into my voice and Gold laughs, he still doesn't get it.

"You really don't know." He tosses his head. "Your mother scores high on the psychopath scale."

"That's no surprise." I stand perfectly still, watching him. He's fidgeting, trying to shake off the pain.

"So, twenty years ago she was one of the women Gold recruited into his breeding programme." He licks his lips. "She agreed to carry two babies created with his sperm, signed a contract meaning she can't disclose the real father and committed to sending regular reports to Gold International. She was also obligated to follow any directions sent by Gold regarding the children." He leans on the chair back. "You know your mother actually tried to save you from Iron Teen?"

Now that does surprise me. "She knew what Iron Teen was? But Lizzie was the one who told us about it…"

"You're such a moron. I can't believe we're related." Gold straightens again. "*We* put the Iron Teen advert on to Lizzie's computer, just like we set up the agency advert last week asking for staff. Lizzie's been our pawn from the start."

"Mother tried to save us?" I catch myself too late. *Ben* calls her *Mum*. I watch to see if Gold is going to pick up on my mistake. He just carries on talking.

"She tried to save *Will*. She said you could go, Ben, but she wanted to keep your brother. Even though she knew how important Iron Teen was to Father, that it was your graduation test. You know, I actually think she developed feelings for Will. You should have heard her rant when she saw the pictures of his body."

"And ... Grady?"

"His situation is different." Gold is holding his broken wrist, talking through the pain. "Doctor Jackson's wife couldn't have children. He agreed to have her implanted with an egg from one of the other women on the programme, fertilized with his own sperm. Grady Jackson is still part of the programme, but he's isn't a Gold."

"So you lured us here to kill us, even though

you know I'm your brother."

"Half-brother."

"And Aikenhead … how many of the kids on Iron Teen were related to you … to me?"

"Ten – one or more on most teams. We lost a lot of our weaker brothers and sisters that week. And in the second run." He shrugs. "Still … brother, half-brother, complete stranger, what does it matter?"

"You're right, it doesn't matter."

Gold blinks. "What?"

That wasn't what Ben would have said. Oh well. I grin and pull my own knife. "Busted."

"What do you…?"

I let the 'Ben' drain from my face, let the chill take over. I must look *terrifying* because Gold actually pales.

"Boo!"

"What the—?" Gold staggers backwards and I lunge with the knife. I knock his weapon out of his hand and it skitters across the floor.

"The thing is, *half-brother* … *I'm* not Ben." I grip his shoulder with one hand almost as if I'm steadying him. He stares into my eyes and I can see the moment he realizes what's happened.

"You thought I died?" I stab once, twice, three times. Hot blood gushes on to my fist. It's immensely satisfying. "Ben would never let me die." I laugh at the look in his eyes. "He's been looking after me my *whole* life. You didn't really think he'd have left the island without me ... did you?"

Chapter Eighteen

Grady

It takes a while for the lights to come on in the music room. The door to the armoury slams shut, but they remain off. In fact, it takes so long that I started thinking something had gone wrong ... and I know how crazy *that* sounds.

The room is as I remember it, apart from the bars over the steps that lead to the games room. The first thing Lizzie does is hobble over and rattle them, but they're padlocked. I assume we'll be looking for that key, as well as the one for the library. Now Lizzie is sitting in a chair, peering at the paper on the side table and holding her left shoulder with her right hand.

The piano dominates the room but there are other instruments around us on stands: a violin, a cello, a trumpet, a flute. A single large bookcase is filled with colour-coded music books.

There are no pictures on the walls here. The

wallpaper is red, patterned with gold, and there is a camera above our heads.

Aanay and Iris are looking at the music books. Bella sits at the piano. Her fingers hover over the keys but she doesn't play anything.

Lizzie looks at her. Even though Lizzie knows what Bella is, even though she's hurt herself and could be paralyzed for the rest of her life, I know exactly what she's going to say.

"Are you all right?"

Bella turns the good side of her face towards her. "You mean because of *this*." She gestures at the other side of her face. The way I'm standing I have a clear view of her bad side. I drift closer.

Lizzie nods. "It must be agonizing."

"It is." Bella tilts her head so that her hair falls over her face. I lose my view of her puckered, blackened skin.

"But —" Lizzie touches the spear in her lap — "that isn't the worst thing for you ... is it?"

Bella says nothing for so long that I think she isn't going to. Then she sighs. "I always knew I was the most beautiful girl in any room." She lifts her hand to her face but doesn't touch it.

"I don't want to be ugly. Ugly people have to deal with things like rules and *consequences*. I've only ever had one person refuse me anything. You want to know what happened to him?"

Lizzie shifts uncomfortably.

Iris looks round. "*I* want to know."

"It was at school. I wanted the status of being with the most handsome boy. His name was Matteo. But Matteo was in love with a girl from his own class." She waves a hand and frowns. "I don't remember her name." She touches her hair then and pulls it forwards, examining it. "Look, it burned my hair too." She holds up a shortened curl and then drops it. "I invited him to our winery. Half an hour after he arrived, when I'd given him a drink, I screamed for Papa. I told him Matteo attacked me."

Lizzie gasps. "Just because he wouldn't go out with you?"

Bella's frown deepens, making her face into even more of a fright-mask. "I told you, no one refuses me."

Aanay stares in horror. Iris says nothing. I lean in closer. "What happened to him?"

"Father punched him so hard he didn't wake up

... he's still in a coma. That's why we had to sell the winery."

"Don't you *care*?" Lizzie limps across the room. "That boy ... and you just ... don't care!"

Bella shrugs. "I care that it taught me a valuable lesson."

Lizzie nods. "That even if you're beautiful, you don't always get what you want?"

Bella laughs. "No. I learned that if you're beautiful, people believe every word you say." She stops laughing. "Who will believe me now, Lizzie?" She lifts her fingers and presses them to the keys, playing a minor chord.

As she plays, the piano lid creaks.

Then it springs forwards, but Lizzie is already moving.

When everything comes to a stop, Bella is staring at the butt of the spear, which is holding the lid millimetres away from her delicate fingers. With a small scream, she pulls her hands back to her chest, just as the lid crunches through the haft, shattering it into splinters.

Lizzie leans on the piano for balance as Bella falls off the stool, clutching her hands to her. "*Merdata!*"

225

I pull Lizzie upright. "How did you know?"

Lizzie points. Once she does, I can see what she had: the mechanism behind the lid.

"Set to go off if someone plays anything," Iris whispers from behind us. "Well done, interloper, you might be useful after all." She turns back to the shelves. "Now shall we stop fooling around and find our way out of here?"

Bella is still breathing heavily, her chest heaving. Aanay steps forwards, instinctively wanting to help her. Then he stops, shakes his head and retreats to the chair Lizzie had left.

Bella picks herself up. She looks at Lizzie, clears her throat and tugs her hair back over her face. "Thank you ... I suppose."

"You're welcome ... I suppose."

I yank Lizzie's broken crutch from the piano and give it back to her.

"Grady." Aanay picks up the paper on the side table. "Look at this headline." He turns the crinkling page to face us.

Lizzie reads it out loud. *"James Moriarty wins Nobel Prize in Economics for work on poverty."*

"Wasn't Moriarty the villain in Sherlock Holmes?"

I look at her. "*You* should remember, you made us watch it with you."

Aanay puts the paper back down. "What else do you know about Sherlock Holmes? Is there anything to do with music?"

Lizzie nods. "He played the violin."

I lift it carefully from its stand. "It looks ordinary to me." I turn it over. "There're no markings on the body."

"Are the strings meant to be different colours like that?" Lizzie limps nearer, her left arm dangling. She looks at the cello. "The cello strings aren't coloured."

"That's true." Aanay is with us now. "Red, blue, green, yellow."

"Or yellow, green, blue, red," Lizzie adds.

Iris is by the bookcase. "The music books are colour-coded."

"You think this indicates one of the books?" Lizzie turns. "Which?"

Iris looks for a moment and then stands triumphantly, wielding a book. "*Sting's Greatest Hits*. It has yellow, green, blue and red stripes on the spine." She opens it to the contents page then glances at Aanay. "You wanted clues with gold in them. 'Fields of Gold' is on page ten." Then she looks at Bella with a cold smile. "By the way, it's piano music."

Bella stands in the centre of the room, her fists clenched. She swallows but says nothing.

Lizzie looks at Aanay. "Do you think we have to play this?"

Aanay touches Bella's shoulder. "I think so, yes."

Bella looks up, dark eyes flickering. "Do any of you play?"

Lizzie shakes her head.

Bella flexes her fingers. "If I hit the wrong note…"

"The piano lid will come down." Lizzie hands me the spear and leans on the chair back. "Grady can jam this in before it hurts you, like I did."

Bella sighs and I stand above her as she sits slowly down on the stool. I raise the spear, holding it horizontal, ready. She carries a sour smell now: burnt skin and hair, sweat. It really is unattractive. And yet I find her more interesting now than I ever did. It turns out I like my toys broken.

Bella cracks her knuckles then thrusts her chest out a little. "You won't let me get hurt, will you, Grady?"

I shake my head. "Not you, Bella."

"You'd better be fast."

"I will be." I consider for a moment what will happen if I'm slow. Bella will lose her hands and she'll be no good to us in any of the other rooms. I decide to be fast.

Iris balances the open book on the music stand. Bella exhales shakily then rakes her hair out of her eyes. Her eyes challenge me to flinch. I don't.

"You can do this."

"It's an easy piece – of course I can." But Bella's voice shakes. She looks at her hands. "My hands are still beautiful, aren't they, Grady?"

"Yes."

"They won't be if you let them get crushed," she snaps. Then she turns to the music. She looks at it carefully. She ghosts the first few notes, not daring to touch the piano. Then she balances the fingers of both hands gently on top of the keys. Tension vibrates in the air. I keep my eyes on the piano lid. There was a creak last time, just before it snapped down. I'm listening for that.

Bella starts to play. She plays slowly, the familiar tune not quite at speed. The notes tremble, but she hits each one firmly enough for the sound to emerge. I strain to hear the telltale groan. What if the lid only made a sound last time because it had been out of use for so long? What if there was no warning this time, just a duff note followed by the snapping of bones?

Bella reaches the second line and there's an audible click. She squeals hoarsely and throws herself off the piano stool, landing with a thud. I shove the spear forwards, but nothing happens. I turn. Bella is on the floor, her legs skewed, and she's panting heavily. I look at the piano. A panel has opened on the side nearest me. I bend and inside there are two keys.

I use the end of the spear to hook them out. "One for the stairs, one for the library?"

Aanay nods.

"Here, you try one, I'll try the other." I toss him the smaller key and look up at the clock. Only half the time has elapsed; we're getting better at these puzzles.

"Grady, this isn't working." I turn from the library door to look at Aanay. He's standing by the stairs. The padlock is open in his hand, but the metal gate isn't moving. He pushes it with a grunt. It only shudders.

Lizzie heaves herself to her feet. "Grady?"

I return her crutch, and she limps to Aanay and tries to pull the gate open herself. She puts her shoulder against the bars and heaves. "It has to open! It has to!" She starts sobbing. "Ben! *Ben!*"

No answer. Iris watches her derisively.

"You realize this means we'll have to go through the library, Iris," I say, wanting a reaction from her. "More traps, more danger. We could have bypassed that if we'd managed to get up those stairs."

Iris stalks to the library door. "Come on then. Are you really that scared of *books*?"

Aanay walks past her. "If you're not, then you've got a real problem."

I take a moment to consider his words. Am *I* scared? I don't want to be injured. I certainly don't want to die. But fear? I can understand the concept. I can see how it looks on Lizzie, on Aanay. Dawson was afraid as he was dying. But me? Bella's not exactly scared either, even with her injuries. I can see her thinking as she walks. She's not frightened. She doesn't know how to be, any more than I do.

Chapter Nineteen

Will

I watch them give up and leave the stairs, then I release the button that was operating the gate. It had been hilarious holding it closed while they struggled. Lizzie's *face*!

In the back of my mind, Ben stirs. He's been quiet for a while now, but I have to be careful when I think of her. It might wake him.

I don't want them in the games room yet. I haven't quite worked out all the controls. Christopher Gold died without telling me how to operate the castle, but I worked out a few things. I've put the automatic arming system on. I also memorized the master codes from Christopher's list. For a moment I was tempted to try and switch the whole thing off and let everyone out. I must be able to do that from here, but there are three problems with that.

One: How would I get Grady if I let him out?

Two: I haven't quite decided how to take down

Gold Senior yet.

I now know that my DNA could be evidence, not only of my survival of the so-called plane crash, but of some sort of psycho-breeding programme. Not to mention Mother will have hidden away a copy of that agreement she signed. Still, I don't quite know what to do with all that yet. I'd like a bit more suffering on Lizzie's camera, something to really nail him to the wall.

Three: What fun would *that* be?

I twist the signet ring that I now wear on my left hand. It still has Christopher's blood on it, but now I know that I'm a Gold, I'm as entitled to wear it as he was and it reminds me that I'm in charge. *I* beat him.

I could spring a trap or two on Grady, the castle rules don't bother *me*, but... I rub Gold's blood between my fingers. It's drying now, flaking off my knuckles, which is a shame because I'd enjoyed the feel of it when he bled: warm and red, like soup; the pulse of it as it throbbed on to me, the smell, like wet copper. I don't want to watch Grady die on a television screen. I want to get my hands dirty. Anyhow, I lugged that bag all this way.

I can lie in wait for Grady in the chapel or, if I feel like it, in the games room. I can bring him back here, break him into little pieces, take my time.

I smile, and this time it's a full smile, more of a Ben smile.

Yes.

I bend down and rifle through my dead brother's pockets until I find his key card. Now I can get back in here any time I want.

They thought the castle was bad when Gold was in control of it.

Wait till they get a load of me.

Chapter Twenty

Lizzie

I think the feeling might be coming back in my toes. I wiggle them as I look up at the thousands of books. Any other time I'd be impressed: I feel a bit like Belle in *Beauty and the Beast*, staring at the Beast's library.

I lean on the spear as I stumble into the light, dragging the dead weight of my left leg. My whole side is numb, and I have to walk by kind of swinging my body from my right-hand side. I'd be terrified if it weren't for my wriggling toes. I'm desperately hoping that this whole paralysis thing is wearing off.

As I turn, giving my camera a good view of the library and the people in it, I wonder if I've got enough to bring down Gold now. We've got the dart from the armoury wall that did this to me, a recording of the spring-loaded piano lid... What'll be in the library? I keep turning.

Perhaps a bookcase is primed to fall on us, but which one? Where is safest in here?

There's an ornate globe in the centre of the room. Aanay is already beside it. I hobble across to him and lean heavily on my spear. He gives me a weak smile and his eyes are watery, exhausted. I try to return his smile. I still haven't made up my mind about him. He seems all right, he genuinely does. But I've been wrong before.

Grady is walking over to us, leaving Bella by the reading table. The light is reflecting in his eyes, making them into shiny discs. I know who he is and he terrifies me. But better the devil you know, so they say.

"Have you seen the staircase up to the top level?" He points. It's a spiral staircase, all dark gleaming wood and elegant lines. I can see it, but there's no way to get to it without going through a barred gate. "There's an alphabet keypad beside it."

"You mean we need to find a word. *One* word in a library of *thousands* of books. In less than one hour." What if I can't make it back to Ben? What if he's lying injured somewhere, waiting for me?

Aanay sighs. "Where is Gold's camera?"

Bella answers him. "On the side of the staircase. See?" The lens glitters at us from the shadows. For some reason, I feel even more strongly as though it's boring into me.

"I wish we could cover it." Then I groan. "I'm so tired."

Aanay nods. "We have to rest. We're going to make mistakes if we don't."

"We can't. We have an hour." Iris joins us in the centre of the room. "That's part of the point of this, don't you think? Keep us moving until we can't. Until we give up and let a clock run down. What do you think? Do we look for books with Gold in the title, or a book by someone called Gold?"

"Could be." I lift my chin. "Off you go."

Iris stomps towards the shelves.

My eyes go back to the globe. Aanay spins it, almost idly, stopping when his fingers reach India. "We used to go to India every summer for four weeks," he says wistfully. "Mumma's family are from Gujarat. I loved it when I was little, but last year Indrani and I said that we were too old to spend four weeks with our aunt and uncle. We insisted on doing Iron Teen instead." He looks at his feet, then up at me. "I know you're trying to take down Gold, Lizzie. But in case we don't get out of here, I want you to know that Marcus Gold has very destructive karma. His next lifetime will be terrible indeed." He keeps staring at the globe, at the image of India, the gold swirl of writing almost mesmerizing. I follow his gaze, not sure what to say to him. Then I bend closer to look at the other countries.

"Aanay!" I point at the writing. "Not all the countries are written in gold, look."

He spins the globe. "India, Russia, Jamaica and Malta. Iris is wrong – we aren't looking for a book after all."

I rub my eyes. I am really very tired and my head aches.

"The passcode could be one of the countries, or a combination of the first letters of the countries." Grady has overheard us and now he's peering over my shoulder. "We can't just guess – you know what happens."

"We won't have to guess," Aanay says. "There'll be another clue."

We search, exhaustion making us slow. Bella doesn't move from the reading table that sits under the darkened window, starlight shimmering through the bars and on to the back of her head. A book is open on the leather tabletop, its marked spine cracked. Bella picks it up. "*A Passage to India*!"

I look at Aanay. "Do you think *India* is the passcode? That seems too easy."

Aanay wrinkles his nose at the keypad. "Shall I try it?"

Grady takes a single long step to the centre of the room. *He* isn't sure. But I want to get to Ben and maybe it *wasn't* that easy – maybe we're just getting better at the rooms, seeing the shape of the puzzles more quickly. "Try it."

Slowly he types in the word. Five beeps. Then there's a single loud, discordant tone and the clock illuminated against the curtains jumps forwards by fifteen minutes.

Bella swears and Aanay jumps backwards. We all look around, rabbits in a trap, even Iris, her eyes flickering from one part of the room to another, looking for the axe that we're sure is going to fall.

Nothing changes. I exhale the breath I hadn't realized I was holding.

"It wasn't *India*." I swallow the lump that has

appeared in my throat. "We could try the other three country names."

"Don't be reckless, Lizzie," Grady says. "In this room it looks like a fifteen-minute penalty for each mistake. We have to get the code right."

I close my eyes. I *am* being reckless. This whole *thing* was reckless. I came here to help Grady take down Gold and now I'm paying for it. Ben could be dying somewhere, and I'm paralyzed. We were never anything more than Grady's stuntmen. He hid behind us on Aikenhead and he's hiding behind us now. I turn from him before I say something I may regret. He's still dangerous.

"What if we look for other books like *A Passage to India*?" Bella asks, interrupting my thoughts. "Books with the countries in the titles."

"It's worth a try," Grady says. "We're running out of time." He heads for a bookcase and starts scanning books. "If you find one, bring it to the reading desk."

The shelf nearest to me is filled with encyclopedias. I balance carefully, pull down the R and turn to Russia, or where Russia ought to be. "The pages have been ripped out."

"Odd," Iris says. "What about India?"

I look. "The same."

"Keep searching," Aanay says.

I do. I peer along a section of leather-bound travel journals, shelf upon shelf of finance books and scientific tomes. This could well be the most boring library imaginable. Then Aanay calls, "I've got *The Jew of Malta*!" He lays it on the desk alongside *A Passage to India*.

I head for what appears to be the fiction section just as Grady wields his own find. "*The Russia House*."

"That leaves Jamaica," Bella says.

I look at the clock. I can't help it, my eyes are drawn to its ticking. Another fifteen minutes have flown by. I drag my numb leg to the shelves, seeking anything with *Jamaica* in the title. Eventually my aching eyes spot it, a tattered book with a marked spine. "*Jamaica Inn*," I shout.

Grady pulls the book down for me. "Well done."

He piles the books together in the centre of the reading table and stares at them. I let my legs fold me into the chair Bella has vacated. My shoulder aches; the wound on it pulls with every movement.

My whole left side is asleep. I want to close my eyes. I put my head down, looking at the pile of books. Then I blink. The spines are all marked! I reach out and rearrange them.

"What are you doing?" Iris glares.

I turn the new arrangement over, so that the spines are facing upwards. The word HALLMARK appears, written across the spines of the four books.

Chapter Twenty-one

Grady

The clock hasn't changed. It is still ticking down and now there are less than thirty minutes to go. We're all standing on the upper level, glaring down at it. Stuffed animal heads surround us, glass eyes accusing our bowed heads. Hunting trophies: an enormous, sapphire-eyed wolf, a mournful stag with huge horns, a tattered fox, a leaping hare in a glass case, an incongruous little bird in a bell jar, a rubber-like salmon pinned to a wall and, finally, a dusty black bear as tall as I am, his fur patchy and ragged, looms from a corner with bared claws.

"It isn't fair," Lizzie mutters. She's rubbing her shoulder again.

"It's still the same room," Aanay says miserably. "So, it's still the same clock."

"How are we going to get into the games room in less than half the time?" Iris looks frustrated, her cheeks flushed. She's gaining colour, no longer made of ice.

There's another alphabet keypad so it'll be a word.

"It won't be *hallmark* again, will it?" Lizzie asks hopefully.

"Don't be ridiculous," Iris snaps.

"Is it worth a try?" Aanay whispers.

Bella shakes her head. "We can't afford to lose another fifteen minutes."

I turn my back on the clock, but it's reflected in the large mirror that takes up almost one whole section of a wall. I notice that Bella has carefully angled herself so she can't see it. "This isn't achieving anything! We need to think."

Lizzie drags herself to the bookshelf nearest to the keypad and starts pulling books out and tossing them on the floor, grunting with pain each time.

Iris rolls her eyes. "What, you think there might be a secret door?"

"Or something written under the books, I don't know." Lizzie hurls a book so hard that Iris has to leap out of the way. It lands at my feet: *The Book of British Birds*.

"Watch it," Iris snaps.

"You watch it." Tears are forming in Lizzie's eyes.

"We're going to find Ben," Aanay says. "He'll be fine."

"You don't *know* that," Lizzie yells. She turns on him. "I can't go home because everyone thinks I'm dead and Gold can't let the world know any different. My dad is *dying* and I can't go to see him, to say goodbye, because if I do, Gold will have me killed and probably him and Mum too." She gasps for breath. "The only person I've got left, the *only person*, is Ben. And he's not right." She sobs and throws another book. "He's not been right since the island. He's all I've got left. He *can't be alone*. Don't you understand? If I leave him alone for too long…" She stutters to a stop.

"What happens if you leave him alone?" Aanay asks carefully.

"He *changes*." Lizzie looks at me. "If he's still alive, he *needs me*. We have to get to him, because if we don't, if he gets overwhelmed, he'll start talking to Will and then…" She pauses. "Then he'll black out."

"Black out?" Bella laughs. "So what? He faints."

"Not *faint*. Black out." Lizzie throws another book, as if talking about Ben has made her even more desperate to get back to him. "He has these

245

chunks of time that he can't remember."

"But he's awake?" Aanay asks, not understanding.

"He's awake," Lizzie says and her whole face screws up. "He's awake, but he's not there. He's not ... Ben."

My mind has stuck on one thing. "He talks to Will?"

"All the time. It's like he's in the room with us, but only Ben can see him." Lizzie's face is white, not with pain, but with something else. I'm usually good at identifying emotions, but not this one.

"Who is *Will*?" Iris has her hands on her hips. Her stance reveals wet stains under her armpits.

"He was Ben's brother," I answer while looking at Lizzie. "He died on the island."

"Then why does it matter?" Iris drops her arms. "Look, I get it, Grady, your 'investigator' is having a breakdown. She wants to be with her mental boyfriend. I'm not stopping her, in fact I'm all for getting out of this room, but this little drama is only wasting time." She narrows her lips. "We have twenty minutes. Any longer and we won't even be able to put a wrong guess into the keypad."

To my surprise it's Lizzie who answers. "Iris is

right." She looks wearily up through her tears. "Leave me alone. Find the answer."

Bella too has grown bored of Lizzie's outburst. She's wandered off along the mezzanine and is now staring tiredly into the beady eyes of the black bear. Abruptly she turns to look at the salmon. Her head goes from one to the other.

"Bears eat salmon, don't they?" she calls. "And … wolves eat stags. They are pairs."

"But there are seven of those nasty things," Aanay says, averting his eyes.

"Yes – an odd one out." I almost want to give Bella a hug. "It's the bird! The fox eats the hare, the *bird* is the odd one out."

"That's the word for the keypad, then." Bella has triumph sparkling in her eyes. She likes to win. "*Bird* – try it, Grady!"

The clock shows eighteen minutes left. "If I'm wrong and we lose another fifteen minutes, we'll only have three left."

"Better do it fast then," Iris says.

I lick my lips and go to the keypad. "B-I-R-D," I speak as I tap the letters in. *Beep, beep, beep, beep.* I hold my breath. A discordant tone sounds.

Then it feels as if a door has slammed on my fingers. Bruising pain. I'm flying.

▼

"*Grady, Grady!*" Lizzie is shrieking my name. I can hear her dimly, as if from down a long tunnel.

"Just leave him." Iris.

"He's dead and we only have *two minutes left.*" Bella.

Now I can feel something pressing hard on my chest in time with Lizzie's cries. It hurts. I want to squirm away, but I can't. My hand hurts, I smell burning. I can't breathe.

Electrocuted … I was … electrocuted. *Bird* was wrong. Of course it was. All the other clues have had something to do with the word *gold*. We're getting tired, making stupid mistakes.

Lips press against mine, breathing into me.

I still can't catch my breath. And there's something else wrong. I don't think my heart is beating. I think … I may be dying.

How interesting.

Chapter Twenty-two

Lizzie

"Aanay has Grady." Bella grabs me, her long nails digging into my bicep. "You can't help. We have to find the right word *now*, or we're *all* dead."

"It wasn't *bird*." I tear my eyes from the tableau on the rug.

Aanay is pounding on Grady's chest. Grady's short-fade haircut is smoking, his arms and legs are flung outwards and the fingers on his curled right hand are clearly burnt. "If it isn't *bird*, what is it?"

One and a half minutes.

"Maybe we weren't specific enough?" Iris says. "Perhaps we need to put in its actual name?"

"How do we find that out?" Bella snaps.

I stare at the floor and then I remember. "*The Book of British Birds*, I threw it earlier. Quick, find it."

The three of us scramble through the pile of books. My shoulder drives spikes of pain through me as

I paw one-handed through the mess I've made.

"It's here." Iris doesn't waste time gloating over her find, she's already flicking through. "What does it look like? Quick."

Bella runs for the tiny stuffed corpse. I glance at Grady; Aanay is bent double, breathing into his mouth.

"Red face, white body ... yellow and black wings."

"Big or little beak?" Iris is flicking madly through the pages.

"Little."

"It's a *finch*." I slide over awkwardly, examining pages over Iris's shoulder.

"But which one?" Iris lifts the book and turns it to face Bella. "Is this it?"

Bella looks, then she nods. "It makes sense."

I try to scramble to my feet but fall heavily on to my left side. I feel nothing. "You'll have to do it, Iris. *Goldfinch*, type it in."

"I might be wrong." We have twenty seconds left.

"Have you got a better idea? Use the end of my stick. Wood doesn't conduct electricity." I thrust it at her.

Reluctantly she stands and starts typing. *Beep, beep, beep, beep, beep, beep, beep, beep.* She hesitates and looks back at Grady. Then she presses the last key. *Beep.*

The door springs open and the lights go out. I can't help but look at the reflection of the clock where it glows in the mirror. It has stopped with two seconds remaining. My heart tries to beat its way out of me.

I look back at Grady. Aanay is still pounding on his chest. I crawl over. "I'll breathe, you do compressions."

Aanay nods. Bella and Iris watch without comment as I tilt his head using my right hand and then pinch his nose closed. I lean awkwardly in the darkness, my left-hand side still unresponsive. Then I put my mouth over his. I exhale into his mouth then pull up. "Come on, Grady, don't give up. You're not going to let Gold *win*, are you?" I count under my breath as Aanay interlocks his fingers and starts to press down. One, two … I get to ten before Grady coughs.

Aanay scoots backwards, his face pale, his eyes wide.

"Grady?" I sag beside him. His eyes flutter

open, bloodshot and confused. Aanay helps him sit up.

He blinks at me. "That was … an experience."

"You almost *died*." I rub my face.

"Did you get it on camera?" Grady rasps. "Were you facing me?"

"I…" I touch my chest. I'd almost forgotten that I was meant to be recording everything. "Yes. I got it."

"Good." Grady leans back against Aanay. "That'll be good television."

"We don't have to go on just yet," Aanay says. "We can rest here between rooms."

I peer into the dark games room, where we were meant to meet Ben if he managed to get through the chapel. There's no sign of him. He might be injured or dying. He could be having a blackout. I close my eyes. I have to get to him. But … I think the feeling might be coming back in my leg. Aanay is right, we're all exhausted. We'll make more stupid mistakes if we don't rest, and I'll be no good to Ben if I'm dead.

"Ten minutes?" I ask. I look at Iris and Bella. In answer, Bella sits on the pile of books.

Iris slides down the wall, her hands between her knees. "Fifteen," she says.

▼

I don't fall asleep. Exhausted as I am, it would be like a mouse taking a nap in a room full of cats. I do rest, though, and now I can move my left leg, at least a little. My arm remains numb, but I can twitch my fingers. The relief would be greater if I wasn't worried that I'd be dead before I get full movement back.

Iris is watching me with narrowed eyes. Rather she is looking at the camera on my chest. "You need to give that to me."

"No chance!" I scoot towards Aanay and Grady, scattering books as I go. I'd been wondering when Iris was going to make her move. This makes sense. I'm exhausted, half paralyzed and Grady is too ill to stand up for me.

Iris looks at Bella. "You want pictures of you like *that* sent to the press?"

Bella stiffens. "No! Hand over the camera."

Grady is still sluggish from the electric shock, but with Aanay's help he sits up. "You don't think

Gold should pay for your face?"

"He'll pay!" Bella says coldly. "But he'll pay by giving me a company and a *lot* of money. What do I get if he loses his business? Nothing."

"Sue him," I cry. "You'll get millions."

Iris laughs. "Have you ever met someone from Gold's legal department? My sister..." She stops. "Never mind, just give me the camera."

"Stay right there!" I hold up a hand, but Iris doesn't move.

"Be sensible," she says, and her voice is as chilly as her blue eyes. "One way or another I'll have it. You might as well hand it over willingly."

It's time to show my claws. I reach under my skirt, feeling for the hilt of the knife, my eyes on Iris.

I forgot about Bella. She grabs me from behind.

"Get it," she rasps. Her cheek is pressed against mine and I can smell her breath, sharp on my face, and the sour stench of her wound: burnt flesh.

I struggle breathlessly but only half of my body obeys, the other half twitches uselessly and then Iris is on me, tearing at my blouse.

"Get off!"

Aanay lurches to his feet. "Stop this, Iris."

He grabs her arm, but she kicks him off and he stumbles backwards.

Grady levers himself up with the side of a bookcase, but it's too late. With a rip of cloth, Iris has the camera-brooch.

Bella lets me go, which is her mistake. My fingers close around the knife and I yank it from the holster, raising it towards Iris. "Give it back!"

"As if you'll do anything with that!" Bella laughs.

"Give the camera back, Iris." Grady helps me to my feet and we lean on one another. He has a definite singed smell. "We agreed we needed a recording to hold over Gold. Leverage, remember?"

"*You* agreed." Iris keeps her eyes on the knife, but she doesn't look worried. "He may well let us out of here if we destroy this. It's proof of our loyalty."

I raise the knife higher. The serrated edge frightens me more than it does her, but I can't let her know that. "If you do that, the only thing you prove is that you're a fool."

"Give it back to her," Aanay begs. "Please, Iris. There are other ways of proving your loyalty to Gold. Lizzie *needs* the recording. She needs it so she can see her father before he dies."

"Oh *puh-lease*!" Iris rolls her eyes. I want to grab the camera back, but I only have one hand and I'm using it to hold the knife.

"Give. It. Back." My words emerge through gritted teeth. I thought I'd only have to show her the knife and she'd accept that I'm in charge. What do I do now? My heart beats more rapidly and sweat drops into my eyes.

In response, Iris drops the camera. As it bounces on the wooden floor, she raises her foot. I twist out of Grady's grip and throw myself forwards.

I tackle her, hitting her in the stomach with my numb side. We land on the floor and the knife jolts out of my hand and skids away.

"Get the camera, Aanay!" Grady shouts, stumbling towards us, but Bella moves faster than Aanay.

There's a crunch, as if she's trodden on a beetle. She grinds her heel into the little lens, smirking.

"No!" I roll off Iris but it's too late. Bella steps backwards. The camera is in tiny, shattered pieces. I see the memory card, though. It's bent, but some tech-head might be able to save the footage. I swoop towards it, but I'm yanked back by my hair. The blade of my own knife touches my throat and I freeze.

"Don't do it, Iris." Grady holds up his hands.

"Why not?" I can feel Iris's knuckles against the back of my neck, where she's holding my ponytail. Her hands are cold.

"We need her. You want to spring every trap *yourself*?"

"I knew it!" I knew there was another reason he wanted me and Ben here.

"Shut up, Lizzie." Grady steps closer to Iris. His knees are trembling, he's not afraid, just feeling the after-effects of the electricity that's coursed through him. "If you kill Lizzie, *I* won't help you any further. Neither will Aanay. We'll go our separate ways. You and Bella will have to do everything yourselves and your chances of survival will plummet."

Iris's grip on me tightens. "She isn't one of us."

"So what?" Grady moves closer. "You've broken her camera, you win. Why waste her when we can use her?" He shrugs. "Keep the knife, you can always kill her another time."

Iris says nothing but a moment later there's a

shove in my back and I'm flying towards Grady, my shoulder stinging. He half catches me and I land with my right hand beside the broken camera. Before anyone can stop me, I palm the tiny SD card and slip it into the holster under my skirt. Then I twist round. Iris is still holding my knife.

"You're a real piece of work, you know that?" I growl.

Iris gestures with the knife. "Get up. You can enter the games room first."

Grady helps me to my feet and Aanay hands me the remains of my spear. "I'm sorry," he says. "I tried—"

"It's OK." I lean on the broken haft and limp into the next room. The knife is gone and to be honest it's a relief. Less so, though, when I consider who has it now, and what she wants to do with it.

The others follow in silence. After a moment the door closes, and the light comes on. We're in the games room, but the real game started hours ago.

Chapter Twenty-three

Lizzie

The funny thing is, I used to love games. When I was a kid my dad never went anywhere without a pack of cards. We used to spend whole weekends playing board games: Monopoly, draughts or backgammon when I was little; Karuba, Talisman or Pandemic when I got older. Mum and Dad would have a bottle of wine and we'd all get snacks. Ben and I wasted hours with *Zelda* on my Wii, but it's been ages since I played anything.

There are shelves and shelves of games here, familiar and unfamiliar. There's a card table laid out as though someone was recently dealt a hand of poker. The table legs are bolted to the ground.

There's also a dartboard, with three darts in it, and a table-football table. A marble chess set sits by a window seat overlooking the woods. Again, a game seems to have been abandoned mid-play. The white side is winning. Black pieces are lined up beside the board, awaiting rescue.

There's a games console set up under a screen by the staircase that leads to the music room. It isn't barred at this end, but I know it's locked at the bottom. There are beanbags on either side of the console. It flickers when Grady approaches, but he can't turn it on.

Gold's camera is above the football table, which is on a platform in the centre of the room. The far door is marked *Chapel* and it has a keyhole. We're looking for a key.

I groan and head for one of the beanbags.

"What do you think you're doing?" Iris snaps.

"Sitting down." I start to fold into the beanbag, but Iris catches my arm.

"No. *You* can look for clues. Bella and *I* will be sitting down."

"Are you serious?" I stare at her. "I'm not exactly quick on my feet right now."

"I don't care." Iris gestures with the knife. "You've had a rest, so get moving."

"Come on, Lizzie." Aanay tugs me towards the board games. "I'll help you look in the boxes."

Grady hesitates. I can see that he's struggling to

decide. Who does he align himself with? If he helps me look for clues, he sets himself up on the weaker side. If he sits down with the girls, that leaves only Aanay and me looking for a way out, and given that I'm moving like an injured sloth we'll likely run out of time.

Eventually Grady drifts over to the poker table, still a little unsteady on his feet, and stares at the cards. Iris lounges on the purple beanbag, using the knife to clean her nails. Bella is beside her, looking like something from *The Ring,* her raven hair sweaty and tangled over her face, her clothes pitted and stained, her eyes burning.

"Get on with it," Iris sneers.

I open one box – it's a mess inside, the pieces shoved back inside any old how. In another, the board is creased and damaged. A third box contains a broken iPad. Someone doesn't like losing. Without much hope of anything happening, I press the power button. The cracked screen remains blank.

All the games are the same: unloved, damaged, pieces missing or tossed inside. I try to think how the clue 'gold' might come in. There are gold pieces to find in Karuba, but I see nothing in the box that looks like a clue.

Aanay goes to the table football and twists one of the handles backwards and forwards. It squeaks. He keeps twisting, almost as if he just can't stop, and the screech winds into my brain.

"Stop that!" Bella growls.

Aanay releases the handle and pulls the football from a hole in the side of the table. He holds it up to show me. It's gold.

Grady limps over. "Let me see."

Aanay hands him the ball.

"It's heavy, it could be real." Grady frowns, examining it. "There aren't any markings."

I've reached the table now. "What's *Anansi*?"

"What do you mean?" Grady's eyes meet mine.

"It's written on this end of the table: A, N, A—"

"I know how to spell it." Grady hands the ball back to Aanay. "Nana told me spider tales when I was little." He almost smiles. "Anansi is a spider."

It's hard to imagine a little Grady listening to his nana's stories. I wonder if his father approved; he always struck me as super creepy.

"It says *Cerberus* at this end," Aanay says, pointing. "What does that mean?"

"Fluffy was a Cerberus in *Harry Potter*." I frown, thinking. "Wasn't he a three-headed dog?"

Grady shrugs. "Never read it."

"Cerberus and Anansi," Aanay says. "A three-headed dog—"

"And an eight-legged spider!" I grin at him. No matter how terrifying this whole thing is, I get a sense of satisfaction when I solve the clues.

"Three and eight and a gold ball." Grady rolls it between his fingers. "Maybe we need to play football. Three goals in one end and eight in the other?"

I don't even look at Iris and Bella, there's no point. They're not part of this discussion and I don't care what they think. It's not as if they're going to help.

Grady indicates the metal handles. "After what just happened, I'm not putting my bare hands round those," he says.

"Two of us are going to have to." I lean my stick on the side of the table. "Unless there's something in here we can wrap the handles with?" I look round the room, stumped. For a moment I don't see anything, there aren't even curtains. Then I realize the card table is covered with green felt.

"Can we cut this off?" I look at Iris. "I need the knife."

She laughs.

"You'll have to do it then. We need the material."

Iris sighs and rises. Bella shifts her legs so she can walk round her. Using my knife, Iris slashes the material free of the table then stands back. I'm forced in front of her and I tense, expecting to feel the blade, but she doesn't move as I rip it off with one hand, raining cards on the carpet. Iris's hack-and-slash approach makes it easy to tear the felt into a rough half. I hand one each to Grady and Aanay.

Grady glares coldly and I twitch the fingers of my left hand meaningfully. "I can only operate one handle. You'd have to do the other one *anyway*."

With a blank expression he hands me the ball, tears his piece of felt in two, wraps his hands and grips the handles on the Anansi side. Then he waits for Aanay to do the same on the other side of the table.

Soon they're both standing on the raised platform like performers, but Aanay looks terrified. His arms are shaking worse than Grady's, which are randomly twitching as though electricity is still discharging through his body. "It'll be all right," I say. "Just put eight goals into Grady's side and Grady will put three goals into yours. You don't have to play properly, just let each other knock the goals in."

Aanay nods. There's something about him that makes me want to protect him, but I fell for that on the island with Grady. I have to look out for myself and for Ben, no one else. I must remember that.

I realize Bella has risen. Both girls are now standing at the other side of the table. They want to see Grady or Aanay hurt. If only I had my knife back. But then I shake my head. Even if I did, what would I do with it?

"Go on then." Iris waves the knife. "Play."

"Who first?" Aanay looks at Grady.

"I'll put one in your goal." Grady looks at the ball I'm holding. "Drop it into the hole," he says. I resist the urge to hurl the gold chunk at his head and release it into play. It thuds into the centre of the table, between the two rows of plastic midfielders and rolls a little towards the blue side.

Aanay doesn't move as Grady knocks the ball forwards. It heads slowly towards the goal.

Heavier than normal, it isn't moving as fast. He has to hit it again with his attacking line. It rolls noisily towards Aanay's goal and Aanay pulls his goalie out of the way to allow the ball to fall in. The moment it does, Grady lets go of his handles and Aanay freezes.

The golden ball rattles into the goal then vanishes. It clatters through the inside of the table until it appears again in the open side.

I pick it up with trembling fingers. "OK?"

Aanay nods. I put the ball back into the game and this time Aanay tries to kick it with his midfield. He misses and Iris sighs loudly, pointedly.

"Shut up, Iris, unless you can do better." I give Aanay a tight smile. "You can do this!"

He gulps and moves his handle again. This time the ball glances off one of the little blue players and skids sideways. "Sorry." Aanay waits for the ball to roll towards the middle and uses his attacker to guide it towards Grady's goal. Grady releases his handles as the ball clanks its way back to the hole, again I pick it up.

"One—all," Bella rasps.

I nod and drop it back into the game. This time

Grady moves more confidently. He sends the ball flying into Aanay's goal before Aanay even realizes what is happening. The ball rolls back into the side and I pick it up.

"Two—one to Anansi," Iris mutters.

I drop the ball in again. This time both Aanay and Grady go for it, they're getting competitive. Grady gets his midfielder to the ball and again it streaks towards Aanay's side. Aanay blocks it with his goalkeeper and knocks it back towards Grady's goal. Grady intercepts with his defender and spins the handle. The ball fires towards Aanay's goal and hammers against the back of the table, before vanishing inside.

"Three—one." Bella taps Grady on the shoulder. "That's all three in the Cerberus end. You can stop."

Grady shrugs her off. "Aanay still has to get all eight goals in my end. Nothing is happening, is it?" We peer around the room; nothing has changed. No panel has opened, no key appeared. The clock continues to tick.

I drop the ball back inside.

Aanay looks at Grady. "Do you want to swap sides?"

Grady shakes his head. Aanay carefully puts a goal past Grady's keeper.

"Three—two," Iris announces.

The next time I put the ball on to the table, Aanay bashes it off the side edge of the goal and Grady is forced to take hold of his goalkeeper and knock it in himself.

"Own goal." I swallow. "That still counts, right?"

Grady nods. "Three-all. Aanay, you just need to score five more."

I smile encouragingly. "You're doing great, Aanay."

This time when I drop the golden ball into the game, Aanay hits it firmly towards Grady's end. The ball rolls smoothly in a straight line. Grady pulls his keeper out of the way and the ball drops into the goal.

"Three—" Bella starts and then she falls silent. My feet start to burn. I look down and shriek. The platform that Grady, Aanay and I are standing on has changed colour. It's now bright red. My wooden crutch is charring, and the smell of burning wood and rubber fills my nostrils. Even through my shoes, my feet are burning.

I throw myself backwards, crashing into Grady. We smash into the floor together.

Aanay is rolling on the carpet on the other side, yelling and holding his feet. Grady's rubber soles have melted, leaving black smears on the platform. He drags his shoes off and throws them across the room. They crash into the window with twin thuds and scatter the chess pieces.

Iris raises her brows. "What did you do wrong?"

"Nothing!" I yell. "We agreed – three goals into Cerberus, eight into Anansi!"

"Then why did that happen?" Iris snarls.

"I don't know!" Grady is glaring at the football table as he stands up. The bottom of it is metal and the legs are glowing, red-hot. If the table collapses, then we won't be able to solve the puzzle. We'll be stuck here when the clock runs down.

Finally, Grady's brows come together. "Anansi was a trickster. He always won by tricking other animals, reversing things back on them."

I frown back. "So, there's a trick here?"

Grady walks round the table. "Maybe we're meant to put eight goals in the Cerberus side, three in Anansi."

"How? We can't get to the table. And time is running out!" Fury and fear have been whirling in my gut all day, a constant low-level nausea that suddenly spills over. "*I'm* not getting back up there."

"You are." Iris shows me the knife but I ignore her.

"Me neither," Aanay whispers. "What are you going to do, stab us all?"

"You're no good to us if you don't do what you're told." Iris stalks towards me then spots Bella and stops. "Gold wants a video of you, Bella, like he has of the rest of us. Maybe if *you* do it, he'll have what he needs from the castle, then he'll let us out." She flips the knife, so the hilt is facing Bella. "Here, take it."

"You want me to kill her?" Bella strokes the blade thoughtfully.

"Wait!" I scramble backwards and realize my left arm is working. I have feeling back in my side. I pull my elbow close to me. Might it help me if they don't know I can move yet? "Just ... find us something to stand on, something to protect our feet and we'll go back up."

"Speak for yourself." Grady sounds bored.

"Fine, *I'll* do it. It only needs one person to knock the ball into the goal." I look at the window. "The chess set – didn't it have a marble board?"

Grady nods.

"I can stand on that."

"Good idea." Grady fetches the board. "You aren't going to kill her, are you?"

Bella is still looking at the knife, tilting it back and forth so that the light strikes her in the face and then shifts off to scatter against the window. "Not yet," she murmurs.

I consider pointing out that I saved Bella's hands, but I don't think it would make any difference. They don't feel anything; let alone gratitude, loyalty or obligation. It's all about what's best for them in that moment, and if Bella decides its best for her that I die … then she'll try and kill me.

I swallow as Grady drops the marble slab next to the football table. He helps me on to it and takes the spear so that I can lean on the top.

I pick up the gold ball. I'm on the Anansi side and I need to kick the ball into the Cerberus goal. But the chessboard isn't that large. If I overreach, I'll fall off. I'm reminded of a game we used to play.

271

Ben and I used to pretend we were surrounded by lava, and would jump across the equipment in the park at the end of my road, yelling to one another that we couldn't touch the ground.

This time the floor really is going to burn the flesh from my bones. I must stay on my little stepping stone. I roll the ball in my palm and find it warm. I pop it into the game and gingerly knock it towards the Cerberus goal. What happens if we're wrong? What's the penalty for another mistake? I resist looking up, wondering if something is primed to fall from the ceiling. I watch the ball roll.

It's skewing sideways; I'll have to use my attackers to push it in and I don't want to show the others that I can use my left hand. I twist on the cool slab, dangerously close to wobbling off. Then I rebalance, take hold of the handle with my right hand, and spin the ball past the blue goalie.

My shoulders tense and the wound on my left side pulls painfully. Nothing happens.

"Does that mean we're right?" Aanay asks.

Grady shrugs.

"Five–three," I mutter. "Three more?"

Aanay nods.

I'm tired and I want this over with. This time when I put the ball midfield, I spin the handle, as Grady had and the ball whizzes into the goal with a smack.

"Six-three," Aanay mutters in a shaking voice.

My neck aches. I'm trying not to look at Bella playing with the knife she intends to stab me with. I put in another goal.

"Seven–three," Aanay whispers. "Last one."

I play the final round and watch the ball roll towards Cerberus. As soon as I know it's going in, I leap towards Grady. He catches me and we watch the ball trundle slowly into the goal. It teeters on the edge. I haven't hit it hard enough. Grady grunts and nudges the table with the charred and broken spear. It wobbles and the ball tilts into the goal. The room is silent apart from its loud progress through the table.

There is a long pause and, finally, a hatch in the side of the platform opens to reveal the chapel key. Iris picks it up.

"There you go, that wasn't so bad, was it?" She heads for the chapel door and Grady's fingers dig into my arm.

Sudden movement makes me turn in Grady's arms. I'm almost too late, but I get my left hand up to block the thrusting knife with my wrist and shove it downwards. Instead of going into my chest, it slices through my sleeve, over my forearm and into my leg.

I scream.

Grady releases me and grabs Bella by her elbows.

"Let me finish her!" Bella growls.

I land on the floor, the breath heaving out of me. I'm regretting getting the feeling back in my left leg: the serrated blade is buried in it, almost to the hilt.

Grady drags a squirming Bella backwards.

"Gold will let us go if I finish her!"

"Don't be a fool!" Grady shouts just as Iris opens the chapel door and the lights go off in both rooms, plunging us into deep gloom.

I must move; I can't wait for Bella to escape Grady's hold and come for me. But there's nowhere to hide. I drag myself towards the chapel, leg screaming in pain, knowing I'm leaving a trail of blood. What if I bleed to death? I already feel chilled and my arms are shaking, but I'm making progress.

And then there's movement in the chapel entrance.

A shape rises like something from the deeps.

"B–Ben!" I cry his name. Thank *God*, he made it into the chapel. Which means he can get us on to the upper landing. I've got the code for the widow's walk, he has the rope. We can get out of here.

"Ben!" I call again.

The shape comes barrelling into the room. But he can't see me; he'd have stopped, if he had.

He doesn't stop running until he crashes into Grady and Bella. I see them in the moonlight as he hurls Bella to one side and shoves Grady towards the music-room stairs.

"There's no point going that way!" I raise my hand. "Ben?" I see him turn and finally realize what I should have known the second he ran past me.

I'm not looking at Ben.

Will's eyes take me in, then flicker to the blood trail I'm leaving, black in the darkness.

"Who did it?" he asks. I point wordlessly at Bella then Iris and he laughs.

"Don't worry, Lizzie," he says in his odd, cold Will way. "I'll be back."

Then he pushes Grady down the stairs.

Chapter Twenty-four

Will

It felt like I had to wait in the chapel forever. I'll be honest, I was planning on snatching Grady after everyone had come through and taking him back into the games room, leaving the rest to die in the chapel trap. But as time dragged by, I figured I could get him into the music room just as easily, with the *added* bonus of being able to push him down the stairs on the way.

Grady yelps very satisfyingly as he falls. It's dark, but I can see him bouncing from stair to stair, flinging his arms out, trying to stop himself.

Smiling, I race after him, taking the treads two at a time.

I'm not the only one. With a cry of horror, Aanay runs after us and I sneer as he barrels towards me, yelling Grady's name. Grady groans.

A little piece of me had wondered if he'd break his neck in the fall and ruin my enjoyment, so I'm glad he's still alive. I turn, stab Aanay in the chest a couple of times, for fun, then I lean over Grady to push the metal bars up into the ceiling.

I kick him until he rolls off the last step and into the music room, then I let the bars drop behind us. There are shouts from above, but no one seems to be following. I'd assumed Lizzie would at least try to come after us, but she's hurt.

I frown. I told her I'd be back for her, and I will. I might not care for Lizzie the way I did Carmen, but she's one of mine and I can't allow other people to break my stuff. Where would the world be if I did that? I just have a few things to do *first*.

I know where Aanay dropped the padlock, I'd watched him do it on the surveillance camera. I pat the music-room floor in the general vicinity until I find it, then I turn, slap it back into place and grin at Grady. "There, no one can disturb us now."

Dazed, he squints past me, trying to see in the dark. "Aanay?"

"Hold on." I skip to the keypad by the door and type in a word. I love being in charge of the castle! The lights come on, but no clock, I don't want a limit to my time here. "There, is that better?"

Grady doesn't take his eyes from the stairs. I peer over his shoulder and through the bars. "Wow, what a mess!" There is blood all over the place, an oil slick of crimson. The boy is trying to breathe, but I've hit at least one lung. His lips move. "Is he trying to say your name?" I look at Grady. "How sad. Was he your friend?" I turn away, bored. Why watch someone I don't know die when I have all this exciting torture planned?

I drag Grady to a chair by his hair and yank him up into it. He moans, his head rolling. Bruises are blooming all over him and I wonder if he's broken any bones. I drop the bag on the floor and pull out the rope like a magician.

"Oops, don't fall off!" I grab Grady as he tips to one side and wrap the rope round him, once, twice, three times. Then I tie it off.

"Will?" Grady says, his eyes slowly clearing. "Lizzie said … but I didn't understand. How is this possible?" It's almost as if he's talking to himself. He looks at me with his head tilted to one side. "Ben's got Dissociative Identity Disorder from his time on the island, doesn't he? He's made a whole new personality to protect himself."

I laugh. "He didn't do it to save *himself.*"

Grady nods, as if I haven't spoken. "Because his whole personality, the one your mother spent years moulding, was centred on looking after Will. Ben couldn't cope with the possibility that he'd failed, otherwise what did that make him? Your existence means that he didn't fail and, bonus, gives him a way to deal with all … this." He uses his chin to indicate the castle. Then he looks back at me. "Really, it would have been odd if you weren't in there. So, if you're *Will* right now, where's *Ben*?"

"Asleep." I put my fingers to my lips. "Don't wake him."

Grady nods and his eyes flicker past me, to the stairs. "You didn't have to hurt Aanay, he couldn't have harmed you." He flexes his fingers. I've left his hands in front of him.

I frown at him. "Do you really care?"

Grady thinks for a long moment. "I'm … not sure. I promised I'd look after him."

"You care because I made you break your promise?" I crouch beside him and pull the bolt cutters out of my bag.

"Ben wouldn't want you to hurt me." His eyes are

279

pinned to the rusting metal jaws.

I laugh. "Ben doesn't care. You think he's OK with what you did to Carmen?" I lean closer. "She was his *friend* and my … well, *mine*. No one messes with my stuff."

I grab his hand, stretch out the little finger of his right hand and pick up the bolt cutters.

Grady holds his breath.

I cut off his little finger.

I can see him trying not to give me the satisfaction of a scream, but he grunts in pain and his whole face screws up. Blood squirts out, covering my chest.

"Wow, look at that." I bite my lip. "Nine more to go and ten toes. Do you think you'll be screaming by the end, Grady? Do you think you'll scream when I cut off your nose?" His finger is lying on the ground between us, curled up like a salted slug. "Maybe I'll alternate." I grin at him. "Little finger, little toe. Big finger, big toe." I bend and pull off his sock.

"Will?" I glance up and Grady stabs me awkwardly in the side of my neck. Whatever it is, it doesn't go in deep, it can't, his hands are tied; but when I try to put my hand up, to pull out the thing he has jammed there, my arm doesn't want to move.

I'm not dying, I can feel the thing embedded between my neck and my shoulder, but there's something wrong. "Why can't I move my arm?"

Grady kicks me and I fall sideways, unable to catch myself.

"I don't know how long the effect will last," Grady says, wriggling. The ropes are coming loose – I didn't tie them well enough. I should have brought duct tape. "Lizzie got the worst of it." He's almost free. "I reckon the longer it stays in there, the worse it'll be."

I can move my left hand. I reach around clumsily and pull at the spike. I can just get a grip.

The blood from Grady's bleeding stump is lubricating the ropes. They drop in a pile at his feet and he reaches for the bag, yanks out the first-aid kid and stands.

"I'm not going to kill you because I need Ben back," Grady hisses. "And I think I know how to wake him." He looks at the library door; the key is still in the lock.

"Don't you dare!" I can already feel my fingers. "Get back here. I'm not finished!"

"You aren't the real Will," Grady says, shaking his head. "He would never have been so *emotional*. You're nothing but a memory."

He stumbles his way to the games-room steps, hesitates, looking at the body of his friend, then breaks the key off in the padlock. As I roll over, trying to get to my feet and roaring his name, he stumbles his way towards the library.

"Don't worry," he says. "I'll be back."

Chapter Twenty-five

Grady

I'm bruised all over and it hurts to breathe. I'm sure my ribs are cracked. I should wrap them along with my finger but I'm losing too much blood. I lurch into the library and pocket the key. Will's going to be after me any minute. I should have taken his whole bag, but it looked heavy and it would only have slowed me down. I ignore the ticking clock, race to the keypad and type in HALLMARK. When the stair gate opens, I stagger upwards.

I wouldn't have believed it of myself, but the reason I chose this route was so I wouldn't have to step over Aanay's body on my way upstairs.

As I go, I tear open the medical kit. I used most of the bandages on Dawson, but there are enough left for this. I hunch against the wall under the snarling bear, tuck the little bag under my arm and wrap the white linen round my mutilated hand. It turns red almost immediately. Agony throbs from the stump all the way up my arm. Who'd have thought that losing a little finger would hurt so badly?

I bite off a curse and look down. The library door is shaking. Will is hammering on it. My mind races. How did he turn on the lights in the music room without turning on the clock? Did he find some kind of master code list? Can he get into the library without the key?

It doesn't matter. Any second now he'll realize that he only needs to use the bolt cutters to remove the padlock, then he can climb the music-room steps and cut me off.

I totter to the keypad like a drunk and hesitate with my fingers over the keys. I was barely conscious when they typed in the code last time. I don't know what it was.

"Lizzie!" I scream her name. She has to be in the games room. "Lizzie, what's the code?"

Chapter Twenty-six

Lizzie

Bella and Iris head into the chapel, taking the key with them and leaving me in the games room to bleed to death.

With tears streaking my face, I clamber awkwardly on to the window seat. Ben is alive, but he isn't Ben. I need to get to him but I'm not sure I can move. I clutch my leg. The pain comes in excruciating waves, one moment overwhelming me, the next making me think it wasn't so bad. Should I try to take out the knife? Years of watching medical dramas tells me it could actually be sealing the wound; that removing it could do more damage. But surely running around with a *knife* inside me couldn't be a good thing. Grady would know what to do, but he isn't here. I wonder where Aanay is. I clench my fists, trying to sob quietly, afraid that Bella might come back to finish the job if she hears me.

We've failed. I have nothing but a damaged memory card that might or might not be useable and that might or might not have something on it that Matt could use to take Gold to court. That's if I can even get out and get the card to Corruption Watch. I lean my forehead on the bars. My head is aching, my shoulder sore, but compared to my leg, I hardly notice them. I haul in a breath, riding the swell of pain and taking the moment of peace.

Raised voices come from the chapel and I hear a crash that seems to go on for a long time and a scream, muffled by the door. I don't smile, but I'm scared that I want to.

Suddenly there's hammering on the door behind me and I hear Grady's voice. *"Lizzie, what's the code?"* He must have escaped from Will. If Will's chasing him, that means I don't need to move. He'll come to me.

"Lizzie!"

I sit up straighter and shout through my tears, hoping he can hear me because I don't want to drag myself to the door. "Goldfinch! Grady, can you hear me? It's *Goldfinch*."

There's a faint beeping and the door bursts open.

Grady falls through, looking like hell.

"Where's Will?" I try to see past him, but Grady's already slamming the door and looking for something to put against it. Immediately the lights come on and the ticking clock appears.

He drags a chair from the poker table and jams it under the handle. Then he turns to watch the stairs behind us. "Why didn't you tell me?"

"I tried." I close my eyes. "I was hoping…"

"Hoping what? That Ben could do this without needing Will to take over?"

I nod. "I thought … *hoped* if I could get back to him… "

"He'll be coming up those stairs any minute. We have to be ready. Can you get Ben to come back?"

"Usually … but today? In this situation? I don't know. What if Ben doesn't *want* to come back?"

"Then we have to get out."

I shake my head. "Iris took the key. We can't go *anywhere*."

Grady stares at me, and then at the ticking clock. "If Will finds us and you can't fix him, we're dead. If he doesn't, then we have an hour left on the clock. Either way, we lose."

Chapter Twenty-seven

Will

I lean my head on the library door. It's solid oak, three inches thick. There's no way to break through it. I look back at my bag, at the blood-covered bolt cutters. Obviously, I could use them to get through the broken padlock and up the stairs to the games room, but … I close my eyes, listening. I hear the distant chime of Lizzie's voice. If I go up there, she might wake Ben and then where would I be?

So, what? I have to lie in wait, *again*? Separate them, *again*? I punch the wall next to the door, leaving an indent with Gold's signet ring, and lurch upright. I'm getting the feeling back in my limbs.

Of course Grady isn't the only one in the castle who needs to learn a lesson. There're those girls as well. I start to formulate a plan. I'll return to the gallery and use the lift to head back upstairs. I might not be able to get to Grady *yet*, but that doesn't mean I can't have a good time. I shoulder the bag, wrap my fingers round the knuckle dusters and start to whistle.

I'm going hunting.

I open the door and peer from the music room and into the armoury with a wide grin. Dawson's body remains in the middle of the floor, but he's surrounded by fallen masonry and one of the girls, the dark-haired one with half a face, is lying beside him in the moonlight with her neck at an unnatural angle. One of her arms is flung over her cheek, the other over Dawson's chest, as though they're embracing. Shards of brick are scattered over the floor and dust fills the air, yet to settle.

I look up, smirking. I knew the chapel would get at least one. There's a huge hole in the ceiling between the rooms and I can see the vaulted roof through the gap. Bella had quite the fall. She might have survived, if she hadn't landed head first.

I call up. "Hey, Iris, are you there?" Her face appears between jagged masonry. "It's Ben, are you OK?"

"Ben?" She looks behind her then she peers back down.

"Is Lizzie with you? If I throw you the rope, you

could tie it to one of the pews and you could both climb down."

"Lizzie..." She clears her throat. "No, she's still in the games room."

I tilt my head. "Why would you leave her behind? Is she all right?"

"She's fine," Iris calls. "Send me the rope."

I have to throw three times before she catches it, then she vanishes with the end. Eventually she reappears. "That should hold."

She puts her hands to the twisted hemp and looks down. "If I fall, you'll catch me, won't you?"

"Of course." I raise my arms and she swings her feet over the hole. Then she hesitates.

"Is that *blood* on your chest?"

I drop my arms with a twist of my face. "Well, yes." I was hoping she'd come to me, but this could be better. "I had to deal with Grady but now it's *your* turn. I know you hurt Lizzie, and that's not acceptable to me."

Saying nothing, she drops the rope and rolls back into the chapel, so I lope through the armoury, leap over Dawson's legs, and use the master code to head into the entrance hall with the bag knocking my spine and bolt cutters digging into my hip. I leap up the two steps from the entrance hall, into the gallery and race past the artwork towards the lift at the end of the corridor.

I hammer the Fibonacci sequence on to the call button while I get my breath back, and grin as the lift descends for me. When the doors open, I step inside.

I watch my reflection in the polished metal of the walls as I go up.

In my mind my eyes are gun-metal grey, but here I'm facing the fact that in reality they're blue. My hair is curlier too, with a wave I never had. The shoulders are broader. And there are other differences: laughter lines, a small scar on the chin that came from a skateboarding accident when Ben was twelve. I look at our hands. These aren't right either. The fingers are too short, the palms too square.

I close my eyes, so that I can't see. I'm *Will*. Not Ben. *Will*.

The door opens and I step out. Iris is right there in the corridor facing me, her blond hair in disarray. She must have solved the chapel puzzle alone and raced here, only to come face to face with me.

She gives a little scream and twists right. The stairs are in front of her and she takes them two at a time. My grin widens. Those stairs are blocked off, she's trapped herself. Now for some fun.

"Ready or not, here I come!" I sing.

I was going to walk slowly after her, as it feels as if it might be more menacing, but halfway down the twisting stairwell, I crack and start to run. I just can't wait to get my hands on her.

I take the last turn and stare. She's just ahead of me, her face a picture of terror, her hand on a wall panel that wasn't there before; and the portcullis blocking off the stairs is rising.

I yell, but she ducks under the rising metal grate and keeps running, heading for the basement. The place she herself warned us all against.

I glance at the panel as I pass it and certain things start to fall into place: Iris's reluctance to help solve puzzles, her lack of concern; she never had anything to fear from the castle.

"Oh, *Iris*!" I call. "You've been a *very* naughty girl."

Chapter Twenty-eight

Lizzie

"He's not coming." Fifteen minutes have ticked past. If he was chasing Grady up the stairs, Will would be here by now. I rub my watering eyes as another ripple of pain twists my hands into fists. "We have to get to him. But even if we had a way out, I can't move my leg."

Grady stands, clutching his ribs, his bandaged hand under his armpit. He frowns at my thigh then goes to the football table and yanks the felt off the handles, piece by piece, careful not to stand on the cooling metal platform. When he returns, he wads two of the pieces together.

"Hold these." He hands them to me. "I'm going to have to pull it out."

"N-no." I writhe backwards, but Grady puts a hand on my shoulder.

"I have to. Or you're stuck here."

I meet his eyes. He still thinks he needs me.

Either to get through more rooms, or to use against Ben … or rather Will. "OK."

"OK?"

I nod and he grips the hilt of the knife. "Say it with me. One, two…"

He yanks before I can say 'three' and I howl as the knife slices upwards, sliding from my leg, the serrated edge butchering my muscles and rattling against bone. I bang my head against the window bars, sobbing.

Grady tucks the bloody blade into his belt and grabs the wadded felt from me, pressing it against the wound.

"I can't sew this right now. It's too deep." He uses the longer lengths of felt to tie the wadded pieces into place. "But Bella didn't hit an artery, or you'd be dead already."

"I don't think I can move." I grip my leg with trembling hands.

"Stay here till I work out where we're going." Grady gets up. He glares at the ticking clock. After a full minute he looks at me. "Did Iris actually lock this door behind her?" He doesn't wait for my answer but goes to the door. He puts his palm on the handle and pushes. The door opens and he bursts out laughing.

I can't help it. My own laughter joins his. Hysterical, pealing.

Across the chapel the door to the upper hall is hanging open. We literally just have to walk across the room to get out.

▼

The first thing I notice when Grady half carries me into the chapel is the hole in the middle of the floor. A rope is tied to a heavy pew and dangles into the hole.

"That's our rope." I'm still leaning on Grady but I push him to move us closer. "How did it get there?"

Grady shakes his head and holds me still. "We don't know why that hole's there."

To our left is an altar covered by a white cloth. Above it, a stained-glass window showing Jesus in a garden being kissed by one of his disciples, who is wearing a gold tunic. I point it out to Grady.

"Doesn't that just seem *insane* to you? Gold has a bunch of kids killed and then goes to pray in front of his own altar?"

"Satanic masses?" Grady suggests and I snort out a giggle, then a gasp of pain.

"It's not really funny." I grab his arm tighter. "I just feel light-headed."

"It's blood loss. Do you want me to put you down?"

I shake my head. "What do you think of the hole in the floor? If the trap's been sprung, shouldn't we be able to just walk out?"

Grady's eyes narrow as he thinks and I sigh, looking around the room again as I wait for him. The floor has odd-shaped tiles, like crazy paving. Each has a gold letter on.

"Grady?" I whisper.

"What?"

"You've seen *Indiana Jones and the Last Crusade*, haven't you?" I point to the tiles and he nods.

"*Only in the footsteps of God will he proceed...* You think one of the others stood on the wrong tile?"

I grip his arm more tightly. "If there's only one safe way across the floor, *any* of them could collapse."

He sighs. "Well, if that's true, we can only get to the door if we stand on the correct tiles."

"In the film they had to spell *Jehovah*, but that's

too easy … right?"

"It can't be GOLD either…" Grady points. "We can't get all the way across in four steps."

"Can we use the pew to get across?" I look at the weighty wooden seat, but there's no way to reach it without treading on at least two of the tiles. I shake my head. "Well, can you work out a word just by looking at the tiles?" There's a J right at my feet, then a G, a T, an R and a P, but there are broadly ten tiles to a row and the first tile could be any of the first two or even three rows. I realize how useless that idea is, and tears fill my eyes again.

"Iris and Bella worked this out, or one of them did." Grady shakes my arm. "It can't be *that* hard."

"You're right." I sniff. "There has to be a clue – something we can see from this side of the room?" We explore with our eyes. "The only thing I can see is the window."

"What is it showing, do you know?" Grady asks.

"I think so." My mind races back over religious studies lessons. "It's the moment Jesus gets betrayed, in the garden of Gethsemane."

"The word could be *Gethsemane*. The G is still intact, they might have trodden on it to go across."

"Then why did they fall?" I lick dry lips. "Did they spell it wrong, or…"

Grady pulls me backwards and helps me lean against the wall. "Stay here."

He heads back into the games room and returns with the last of the chairs. Then he throws it at the G tile. It smashes through and I scream as the tile explodes and chair, tile and brick crash down into the armoury below.

Painfully, I kneel to look through the hole. My heart is pounding. "Grady, it's Bella." I scoot back from the drop. "She's the one who didn't make it."

"Good," Grady says almost absently. He's staring from the tiles to the window and back again. "The J didn't break. The chair hit both the G and the J, and the J didn't break."

"You think the word could just be … *Jesus*?"

"Or it could be Jehovah after all."

I use the wall to get back to my feet. "Well, we have to find Ben."

"Wait!" Grady yells, but I limp forwards, putting my weight on the J. It holds.

"Idiot!" He exhales. "You could have let me go

for more furniture."

"There isn't any more." I look at him. "The card table's bolted down, remember."

"Now we know why." He's looking past me at the floor. "You can't reach the E from there." He points. The nearest E is all the way over the other side of the room. I'd have to leap like an Olympian to reach it. If I miss, I'll be through the floor.

I look at the gaping hole two rows in front of me. "I wonder what letter was on *that* tile."

"You think another E?" Grady tugs at my arm and I step backwards to safety. "The word can't be Jesus or Jehovah, but we know it begins with J."

My eyes flicker back to the window. "It shows the moment Jesus was betrayed, right?"

Grady nods.

"Jesus was betrayed by *Judas* for thirty pieces of silver."

Grady licks his lips. "But where's the gold?"

"What do you mean?"

"Gold has been a clue in every room. Judas's betrayal was for *silver*. Don't we need to find something gold?"

I shiver. "Silver's *like* gold. It's a precious metal, right?"

"Are you willing to risk it?"

"I ... don't know." I stare at the image. "He's *wearing* gold," I say eventually. "Judas, I mean. In the picture."

Without taking his eyes from mine, Grady nods and steps on to the J. "I'll go first this time. You're too unstable, you might fall by accident. Take my hand."

"Are you sure about this?" I grip his fingers. His bandage is rough against my skin and he winces. "Judas wearing gold," I whisper. "Is that ... *enough* of a clue?"

Grady ignores me. The U is two rows away from the J and to the right. "I'm going to have to jump to the next letter," he says coolly.

"Or through it," I whisper.

He looks at the altar one more time. "There's no other tile it could logically be," he says. Then he jumps. He lands with a wobble on the U and the tile holds.

I exhale an explosion of breath. "Well done!"

"Can you reach my hand?" He reaches backwards, and I step on to the J and stretch forwards. My left leg screams and I wobble, but I can just grab his fingers. I clasp them in mine.

"We're going to have to move at the same time," Grady tells me. "I'll step to the D, while you jump to the U."

I nod and he starts to count.

"Wait – we're going on three, right? Not *two* this time."

"On three. One, two, three." As his feet leave the U, I jump forwards. He lands on the D and I hit the U at the same time. My teeth go through my lip and I taste blood.

"A is next." Grady scans the floor until he finds it, two rows ahead and to the right. "It's even further. I might have to let go."

"Don't you dare!" I cling on to him. My leg is trembling wildly. It's going to collapse, and if it does I'll fall. The sight of Bella staring sightlessly upwards is burnt into my retinas. "We'll have to go faster. One, two, *three*."

I push off with my good leg, but that means I have to land on my bad one. I shriek as I come down with one foot on the D, then I stumble, putting my heel on to the Y next to it. The tile shatters and my leg is dumped into thin air. Grady yells, trying to keep his own balance as mine goes.

I land with one leg and most of my body on D, clinging on for dear life to Grady's hand and the tile edge.

"I have to let you go," Grady grunts. "I'm losing my balance."

"No!" I try to keep hold, but he pulls his hand from mine. I scream again as I start to slip, but dig my nails into the crack between the D and H tile.

"Can you reach my hand?" I open my eyes to see that Grady is now kneeling on his tile, reaching for me again with his good hand.

I swallow and shake my head. The armoury floor is sucking at me. I'm going to land beside Bella. I'm going to break my legs, or my neck, like she did.

"Lizzie, you're a climber, you've been higher than this with worse handholds," Grady snaps and I look at him.

"You're right!" I close my eyes. I was panicking but that's ridiculous. I have a handhold here. I can take my weight and reach for him at the same time, then I can swing my leg up. I centre myself, release one hand and stretch it towards Grady. He catches my hand and helps hold me steady as I swing my leg up and gather my balance so that I can crouch on the tile. Blood drips through the felt on my leg. I let Grady go and tighten the wrapping. The baize is stained deep purple from my blood.

"One more jump and then we're home free," Grady says.

I wish he was right. I wish we were home free, but it's one more jump and then we're facing the next torture chamber. We stand and jump and then again until we're both across the floor.

I say nothing as we hobble into the upper corridor, leaving the door hanging open behind us.

Chapter Twenty-nine

Will

Iris reaches the basement ahead of me and sprints for the furnace room. I'm faster than she is but she has a head start. She keys in a code, slips inside and slams the door on me. I give the door a bang, mainly because I think it'll make her jump.

The basement is windowless and cold. I look to my right with a grin. There's a real oubliette there, a hole covered by a padlocked grate, going deep underground where past Golds would have thrown their enemies to be forgotten about. Beyond that, an actual dungeon. I'd love to see inside, but first … I key in the master code and the door to the furnace room opens.

The furnace itself is more of giant boiler, chugging as it heats the castle, steam rising through a vent from the condenser on its side. Iris is standing to the right of it, by the coal chute, in front of another open wall panel and under a single dim bulb.

She turns as I enter the room, gives another scream and presses her hand on to the panel. I lunge forwards, but nothing happens. I hesitate. What is she expecting here? I frown, looking around, and she slaps her hand on the panel again. Once more nothing happens. Iris yells her frustration, scrubs her hand down her dress and tries again. Still nothing. She grabs the handle of the coal chute and yanks at it wildly.

I step right up behind her. "What's meant to happen here?" I put my hand over her shoulder and help her pull the handle. "Is it meant to open? Should you be able to get out?"

Iris shrieks when she feels me at her back, her knees collapsing and her legs sagging. Then she scuttles out from under me and starts waving desperately at the camera. "Christopher, *Christopher*, let me out!"

I watch her, fascinated. She really does look like Christopher and, I suppose, a lot like me. She has Ben's blue eyes. Or maybe they're Gold's.

"Why do you suppose your palm print isn't working?" I raise a brow. "Did you come to the castle because you thought you were safe? Did Daddy dearest tell you there was a way out, just for you?"

"Daddy dearest?" She widens her eyes and tries to look innocent. I roll mine.

"You're a Gold, right? Iris Gold." I lick my lips as her eyes dart around desperately, looking for a way round me. "You were raised here, weren't you? Upstairs, that's *your* bedroom, *your* games in the games room, *your* piano in the library. You ate meals in that dining room."

Her eyes go to mine and then flicker away again. "Only on special occasions," she muttered eventually. "Usually we ate in the kitchen."

I grin at her. "Daddy was never going to just let you out of here. He doesn't care any more about you than he does about his other little psycho-babies, the ones he had killed in Iron Teen. *You're* being tested too."

"That's not true." She retreats a step and I follow; I like the smell of her fear.

Her fear... I lick my lips, then I pause. Her *fear* – she *isn't* like me. She isn't like Bella, or Grady. She's like Lizzie, like *Carmen*.

"You're not a little psycho-baby, though, *are* you?" I grin. "That's why you're here, *that's* why

306

you're being tested, you're *defective*!"

"No!" she yells. She tries her palm print again, yelling Christopher's name.

"Don't bother." I yank back her arm. "I killed him ages ago."

She whirls. "What do you mean? That's not possible." Then her eyes go to my hand, to my finger, to the signet ring I'm wearing, and they widen still further.

"The room behind the lift," I say, wiggling my finger.

She gasps. Then she starts to laugh, sagging in my arms. "Oh my God, Christopher is *dead*? You have no idea what you've done!"

I frown.

She continues to laugh. "You can't know how many times I wished he was dead. How many times I wished them all dead! Him *and* my sisters. Helen runs the legal department and Victoria is head of acquisitions. They're … *remorseless*, soulless, evil!" She throws her head back. "The things they used to do to me. Father said I had to *toughen up*. That's what this was. He was *toughening me up*. He thought he could *make me* like them. He never meant to let me out … did he?" She looks at her hand as if it's a broken piece of machinery. "I was either meant to die in here or come out as hard as Helen." She swears again and I stare at her.

"You know I'm planning to kill you?"

She stares right back. "I don't much care, in fact I'm happy – if I have to die, at least Christopher isn't walking out of here either. Father is going to be furious about that. Christopher is his heir." She exhales and her whole body seems to lift. "I don't have to pretend any more. I don't have to be this ice person, burying every feeling, every thought in case someone hurts me." She gives me a tremulous smile. "I don't have to be afraid of Christopher."

"Shut up. I'm not your hero." It's my turn to step backwards.

"Ben!" Lizzie's voice. I clap my hands over my ears. She's heading for the basement. How has she got out of the games room? I'd thought she was safely trapped there.

"Ben!" Grady this time. They're together. I press my hands harder against my ears, feeling *him* shifting inside me.

Footsteps pound in the corridor outside. I whip

round to find Lizzie and Grady in the doorway. There's a trail of blood down her leg and her face is dead-white. Her blond hair is stiff with blood: she's been running her hands through it.

Grady is holding his hand to his chest. He's managed to bandage it. I lunge forwards, trying to get my hands around his throat, and Grady shoves Lizzie into me. She gasps and grips my shoulders before she can fall. I try to push her off, but she clings on.

"Ben, are you in there? You have to wake up!" She twists to keep her eyes on mine, and I squeeze mine closed, as if she's the monster under the bed.

"Shut up, Lizzie, go away!"

Lizzie?

No! He's pushing his way forwards.

"Leave me alone, Lizzie. He needs me."

"He *doesn't!*"

I open my eyes. "He does. You think Ben could have coped with all this? He'd never have got the lift working, never have been able to fight Christopher."

"I'm sorry. You're right." Lizzie frowns at my mention of Christopher, but she's focused. I can't throw her off. "He *did* need you, but I'm back now and so is Grady. We'll look after him."

"You're injured." I look at her leg. "And Grady killed *Carmen*."

"I know." Lizzie looks at Grady, who has retreated to the doorway and is leaning against the frame, watching. "And that's not OK. We'll find a way to deal with that, but now isn't the time to be fighting among ourselves. We need to work together. We need *Ben*!"

He can hear her voice, her pleading.

"*You* can't look after him. Only *I* can look after him. He needs me."

You need me.

I need you.

That's right.

But Lizzie *needs* me.

And he's awake. My head pounds and I stagger backwards, vision swimming. Someone catches hold of my arm, steadying me, but I can't see and then…

Chapter Thirty

Ben

Lizzie is right there.

"Lizzie!" I want to throw my arms round her, but … what has Will done? There's a black hole in my memory. She's hurt. What if she doesn't want me to touch her?

As my mind races, Lizzie grabs me and holds me tightly. I bury my nose in the smell of her hair, the warm scent is almost buried under the odour of sweat, blood and fear, but it's there and it steadies me.

Eventually I straighten and look at Grady. "I don't suppose you've found the way out?"

He shakes his head. "We have to keep looking."

Lizzie puts her arm round me and tugs me towards the door. "Leave Iris behind."

"Wait!" Iris runs forwards.

Quickly Grady steps between us, pulls a bloody knife from his belt and holds it up. She has to throw

311

herself to one side to avoid impaling herself.

Gulping, she holds up her hands. "I won't hurt you. I—" She looks at me as if I can help her. Did *Will* get her loyalty somehow? What did he do?

I have a flash of a blond man lying dead in a room. Is it real? I shake my head.

I try to think of something to say that won't give away the fact I have no idea what's happened between them. "What do you want?"

"I-I know the real way out. I heard Christopher telling Father that they were running scenario *three*. That's the oubliette."

"Father?" Lizzie stares at her. "You can't mean … Gold?"

Grady stiffens. "Iris *Pyrite*." He looks at Lizzie. "Pyrite is fool's gold, she's been laughing at us all along. She's always known the way out." He curls a lip. "And that's why you were worried about burning the tapestries in the dining room – they're family heirlooms. We sent your inheritance up in smoke – that must've upset you." He shakes his head. "I can't believe I didn't work it out earlier. I can't believe I didn't see it. It's obvious. You even look like him, like Gold."

Lizzie blinks. "And now you're helping us?"

"Father lied to me. He told me I had a way out – through the coal chute, but..." Iris drags her hands through her hair. "I'm as trapped as you are. *He* killed Christopher, so there's no one watching right now. I can help without being afraid of what will happen."

Lizzie's eyes search mine. "Will killed *Christopher*?" she says quietly.

I shrug. "Who's Christopher?"

"Gold's son." Grady smiles coldly. "You're saying he was here the whole time?".

Iris nods. "He's in charge of running the game. I knew he was watching me. I couldn't do anything to help you. But now..." She runs to the boiler and opens a gold hatch, inside is a puzzle box. She looks at me. "Put your finger here." She points to a little knob on the side.

I offer my finger, but Lizzie hangs on to my arm. "What if she's lying?"

"What if she *isn't*?" I put my finger on the box. Iris *twists* and a wooden rod jumps out. She takes hold of it, turns it downwards and another rod appears out of the top. She presses it and it clicks into place. "You can let go." She twists the whole thing in the middle and it comes apart, then she holds it out to me. Inside is a key. "That'll get you into the oubliette."

"You mean get *us* into it." Grady waves the knife. "You made Lizzie do everything before. Now it's your turn."

I can't argue. I don't know what Iris did to Lizzie, but if Lizzie doesn't trust her, that's enough for me. I let them herd Iris out ahead of us.

The floor beside the oubliette is damp and there's a dank stench emerging from the whistling hole. No light came on this time, but Grady handed me the UV torch, and I'm holding a faint blue glow on the metal cover. A camera is trained on my back but now I know there is no one at the other end of it, watching, it's just a glass eye. I unlock the padlock, throw the bolt and then Grady helps me pull off the metal cover. Underneath, a ladder leads into the darkness.

"I can't climb that." Lizzie looks apologetic. "Not with my leg."

"I wouldn't ask you to." I look at the ladder and then at Grady. "I suppose you're going to claim your hand is holding you back."

"And my broken ribs, actually, thanks," Grady says coldly.

I look at Iris. "It's you or me."

"No." Grady pushes me to one side. "This time, we've got the knife. It's *her*."

"It's all right, Ben," Iris mumbles. "I'll be OK."

I look sceptically at the slippery rungs, rusty and slimy with mould. "That doesn't look safe."

"Hold on!" Lizzie says as Iris puts her hands on the top of the ladder and prepares to swing on to it. She looks at Grady and then back at Iris. "I can't believe I'm asking this, but … are you prepared to testify against your father?"

Iris stares at Lizzie. "You mean … go to court?"

"Yes."

"But … we destroyed your camera and my family has all the money in the world. They'll discredit us. No one will believe anything we say."

"Actually…" Lizzie pauses, sighs and looks at me. "There was a second camera. Ben was recording the whole time." She points to my shirt, at the button that is slightly bigger than the others. "There must be *something* on there that we can use, if we cut out the footage of Will, I mean."

Grady looks vaguely impressed. "Lizzie's brooch was a decoy?"

I nod.

"Dangerous, but clever." He puts a hand in his pocket and pulls a notebook from his trousers. "We also have this. I was going to contact Ian King and let him know what happened to Dawson. I figured if we couldn't take down Gold one way, King might take him down another."

"So, we have at least *some* footage to back up our story, Dawson's notebook, which should get us the ear of Ian King, and we have you." Lizzie grips Iris's shoulder. "It could be enough." Then she looks at Grady. "But when we get out, Gold is bound to be waiting for us. We had thought Ben and I would be able to sneak out and escape to the beach – we've got a kayak waiting. But there's only one exit and Gold knew we were here the whole time so … we can't escape."

Iris clenches her fists. "You're wrong. If Christopher *is* dead, then we have a chance. It's not like Father is camping in the forecourt. In the past, these games have taken anything from a few hours to a few days." She swallows. "He's in the Gold Hotel in Inverness, waiting for Christopher to let him know when the survivors reach the oubliette. There's always been a telegraph office in the hotel, linked to the castle. It's been a few years since they've opened Stowerling, but from what I remember, Christopher sends a telegram to the concierge; Father has his men helicoptered in to pick up the survivors and then the footage of the game is transferred to his private office."

Lizzie grabs her hand. "Are you saying that if we get out now, there might not be anyone waiting for us?"

Iris shakes her head. "There'll be a couple of guards, but they won't be expecting us. We could take them by surprise?"

I look at her. "You're Gold's daughter. They know that, right – they know *you*?"

"Yes, I think so."

"So, what if you go out first and call for help? You say we made you open the coal chute at the back of the castle and that we're escaping. We wait for them to go after us, then we leave through the front."

Grady narrows his eyes. "She's betrayed us before. She could be wrong about the guards, or Gold might have changed tactics this time, seeing as his daughter is in here."

"There's no reason for you to trust me." Iris sighs. "But Christopher's death changes everything. They didn't plan for Ben."

"You're wrong, they *did* plan for Ben." Lizzie smiles at me. "They didn't account for *Will*."

I press my fingers against hers and look at the faces around me. "Before we can get out, someone has to go into the hole." I shine the torch downwards. "You can't go down there, Lizzie, neither can Grady, and we need Iris."

"I won't let *you* go." Lizzie frowns. "So, now what?"

Before I can argue with her, Iris stands. "*I'll* go," she says, her face resolute. "I'll be all right. I know what to do." She climbs on to the ladder. "There's a hole in the wall about halfway down, that'll be where the answer is. Christopher once locked me inside for three hours. I was four, but I remember the hole. I thought it was a way out. I was wrong."

She was four years old and her brother shoved her down an oubliette? Will did some awful stuff to me when we were kids, but Dad was usually there to make sure things didn't go too far, and when he wasn't, well … I was bigger and older and mostly I could stop him. By the time Will was six, he knew I was there to watch out for him and that hurting me didn't make sense. I couldn't imagine living in a house with three older psychopathic siblings and insane parents who didn't care what they did to you.

"No wonder she's messed up," Lizzie whispers, but I don't look at her. I'm watching Iris climb, training the pathetic little UV torch on her hands, trying to help her see.

Her foot slips a couple of times, but she manages to keep her grip on the rungs until she gets about halfway.

"It's here, the hole," she calls. Then she falls silent.

"What is it?" Grady yells.

"There are … two holes." There's confusion in her voice. "They've changed it."

"What do you mean?" Lizzie leans forwards, trying to see. I have to wrap an arm round her shoulder to prevent her toppling into the oubliette herself.

"There are two holes, and each has a handle." Iris looks up. "One is gold, the other is silver. I–I guess I have to pull the correct handle."

"It has to be the gold one…" Lizzie looks at Grady. "Doesn't it?"

"The clue has been 'gold' all the way through," Grady says. "But the thing is … if I was setting up the game, I'd play one final trick. I'd make sure the players thought that gold was the answer by making it so all the way through and *then*, when they got confident, I'd turn it back on them." He looks at me. "Will would say the same."

I tighten my grip on Lizzie. "What do you think?"

"I don't know. Maybe we're meant to think that. I mean most of the people getting to this point … they'd be psychopaths, wouldn't they? They'd think like Grady. So, the best way to trick them into pulling the wrong handle … would be to not play a trick at all."

I shine the torch on Iris. "Grady thinks the gold is a trick. He says you should pull the silver handle. Lizzie thinks you should pull the gold."

Iris sighs loudly. "What do *you* think?"

My head starts to pound. I can feel Will again, pushing to take over, offering to let me out of this decision. "They've both got good points. You know your father best, what would he do?"

Iris stares at the wall for a long time. Then she reaches into one of the holes. Her arm disappears up to the elbow. "I'm pulling the gold handle," she calls. She pins her eyes on mine and she pulls.

There is a loud clank and she screams. Her whole body goes limp and her feet slip on the bars, but she is held in place by the arm that is jammed into the hole.

I hear the whirring of machinery, like a blender or a garbage disposal. Iris is still shrieking. Lizzie grips me hard enough to leave bruises, screaming herself. Grady takes the torch from my shaking hands and holds it steady.

Then, finally, Iris's arm comes free. Her hand is gone, in fact there is little left beneath the elbow. Blood spurts and the faint light picks out jagged shards of bone beneath the sleeve of her dress. Lizzie screams again and Iris sags; she's going to faint.

I push Lizzie off and swing down the ladder. I reach Iris just as she falls. I cling to the bars with my hands and wrap my legs round her waist. She tips backwards into me, unconscious, her tormented face flecked with blood.

I yell at Grady. "I need help here."

"There's not much I can do," Grady calls. "We haven't got the rope."

"I'm *not* dropping her. We need her, Grady!" Now I'm holding on with one slippery hand, the other is tangled in Iris's collar and hair. Sweat stings my palm and rust flakes prick my fingers.

Lizzie vanishes. When she reappears, she has our rucksack. "Do you think you can get this on her?"

I press my forehead against the ladder, focusing on holding on, as Grady descends with the bag.

When he's reached us, I tighten my thighs round Iris and open my hand. She drops a few inches, but I hold her. Then I reach up, take the bag and loop one strap around her left arm. Somehow, I manage to get the other round her right shoulder. It isn't easy, and by the time I've done it, my fingers are slick with her blood. When I'm sure it's secure, I grip the carry handle on the top of the bag and unwrap my legs slowly. The sound of popping stitches is like gunshots in the mouldy air, but the handle holds.

I start to haul her upwards.

As soon as he's able, Grady reaches down to help, and we drag Iris on to the top of the oubliette.

Lizzie stares at her mangled arm, then she tears off her own blouse and wraps it round Iris's stump, until there's nothing to see.

I drop back on to the ladder. "I'm going to pull the silver lever."

"Wait!" Lizzie shouts. "What if they were *both* traps? What if no one is meant to get out of here alive?"

I hesitate with my feet on the rungs. "It's a risk we have to take."

"No!" Lizzie's face appears in the circle above me. "You can't."

"I have to. Iris said—"

"Iris could have been wrong. They might have let her overhear them, deliberately misleading her. What if the way out is really through the dungeon, or the servants' quarters or somewhere? Why don't we go back for our rope and go out through the widow's walk?"

I pause again, the sound of the machinery in the hole grinding in my memory, but I keep climbing.

"You can't climb this ladder, so you *definitely* can't climb a rope. Iris is unconscious. Grady has broken ribs and only one good hand. I can't carry all of you and that's if our rope is even long enough to reach the ground. It has to be this way." I stop when I reach the hole. It's almost too dark to see inside. The gold handle is no longer gold; it is slick and red and spattered with gristle and little pieces of bone.

"Ben, *please!*" Lizzie screams. "If you're wrong, how will we get you back? You'll be stuck down there. We'll never get out."

I thrust my hand into the hole and take hold of the silver handle. Gold's signet ring glitters at me. I wrap my fingers firmly round the bar.

"Ben!" Lizzie cries. "I-I love you!" I look up and she hesitates, then she carries on. "I haven't said it before. I wasn't sure how you'd take it, because it's my fault Will's dead … if I hadn't made us do Iron Teen."

"Lizzie, I don't blame y—"

"Listen to me." She leans over the hole. "You don't have to say anything. You just need to know… You're a package deal, Ben – you and Will. I've always known that. And that hasn't changed.

If we get out of this, it'll be because of Will. *He* saved us. Maybe one day you won't need him any more, but until that day, I'll live with him too. Just … don't die, OK?"

My heart fills with something more than love; it's relief too, because I'm not going to lose her. Inside me, Will stirs and then settles. "I love you too, Lizzie," I say.

Then I pull the handle.

Chapter Thirty-one

Grady

When Ben gets back to the top of the ladder, he's holding a key. It's much bigger than any of the others we've found, which, I reckon, bodes well. I raise an eyebrow at Iris, who is starting to stir. She should have listened to me and pulled the silver lever.

Ben is looking at Lizzie as if he's going to kiss her, but to my relief he hands her the key instead, then lifts Iris on to his shoulder.

I offer Lizzie my own arm and we lurch out of the room housing the oubliette, leaning on one another. I turn towards the stairs, but Ben shakes his head and leads us to the lift. He presses the button with his free hand, once, once again, then twice, then three times.

I frown. "The Fibonacci sequence?"

He nods. "Will worked it out… I remember him talking to me when he did it." The lift doors open, and we stagger inside.

"Is Will talking to you now?" Lizzie leans against the wall as the lift starts to rise.

Ben shakes his head. "Not exactly talking … but he's here." He says nothing more about it.

When we reach the ground floor, the doors open and we spill out into the gallery. It feels like forever since we worked out that the codes were on the paintings. Even longer since we arrived, but it was only yesterday. We've been awake for twenty-four hours, exhaustion is like sand in my bones. Three people have died. Sunrise filters in through the window bars, making the parquet flooring shine.

I lead us to the main door and Lizzie holds up the key. "Do you think there'll be one more trap?"

I shake my head. "Just Gold's guards outside. We can't open this until Iris wakes up, though. She has to go out first."

We sit, leaning against the door, trying not to fall asleep as we wait for Iris to come round, twitching and moaning in pain.

Eventually she leans over and throws up, spattering the floor around us with vomit and bile. Lizzie holds her hair out of her face. She's colourless from blood loss.

"I'm so sorry," Lizzie says. "But you have to go out first, to send the guards away."

Iris nods, jerkily. Ben helps her stand and puts the key in the lock. Lizzie and I move to one side. Lizzie holds her breath as Ben turns the key, but nothing happens.

He puts his shoulder to the bar and pushes. It lifts, the door opens, and Ben steps to the side to stand by Lizzie.

Iris staggers into the light.

We don't dare try to watch her, in case we're spotted, but we can hear her crying, telling the guards that we forced her to open the coal chute for us and that we're escaping out the back.

Somebody says something about her brother and Iris replies that she doesn't know why he hasn't alerted them. She begs them to hurry. Says she needs a hospital.

A moment later she appears in the doorway once more. She nods at me, and then collapses.

Ben catches her, and Lizzie and I stagger out of the door beside them, blinking in the sun.

Automatically I look around, but our ruse has

worked, the guards are gone. Before us, steps lead to a long gravel driveway and to the left, signposted with a carved stone, the path to the beach. The air is fresh and still and birds are flying overhead, dark commas on the brightening sky.

Lizzie starts to cry.

Ben leads us towards the beach path. "We've got a kayak. We'll get out to sea and call Matt on the sat phone as soon as we're out of Gold's dead zone."

"Don't call it that," Lizzie whispers.

We make our slow way down the coastal path, feet crunching on stone. Iris bounces on Ben's shoulder. Lizzie pulls a packet of pills out of her skirt pocket and hands them to me.

"Sleeping pills?" I frown.

"Let's keep her that way." She nods towards Iris. "At least until we can get help. We can't take her to the nearest hospital, Gold will find her. We'll have to get her somewhere she won't be known, give them a false name ... I don't know."

I hadn't even considered what would happen if Gold got his hands on his daughter. Right now she's our best chance of taking him down, so she has to stay hidden.

When we get to the beach, I stare at the water. On Aikenhead, the sea had held us trapped. Now it offers freedom. I help Ben dig the hidden kayak out of the sand and drag it to the surf.

"I can't believe he isn't watching us." Lizzie stares upwards, as if expecting a camera drone to fly overhead. There's nothing but the crying of the gulls.

It's tight, cramming all four of us in a craft built for two, but it floats and we push off. Ben starts rowing and we move beyond the headland. Finally, the sat phone gives a loud beep and Lizzie holds it to her ear. "It's ringing!" She looks at Ben. "I'm calling Matt."

It rings for a while but eventually someone picks up, I hear the soft burr of their sleepy voice as Lizzie talks rapidly into the receiver, telling our story. The sleepy burr develops a sharpness, but I can't hear what they're saying and then Lizzie hangs up.

"He's sending the coastguard." She looks at Ben, eyes shining. "He's meeting us in Aberdeen."

I look at the two of them and my heart starts to sink. If they think Gold didn't know about the kayak and isn't monitoring the coastguard, then they're not as smart as I thought.

▼

Maybe I was wrong. Perhaps he was still in the hotel spa, getting a Swedish massage, when we were picked up. He might have been having dinner in his Michelin-star restaurant, when we were all (except Iris) sitting in a poky office, eating McDonalds and watching back the hastily edited video from Ben's camera.

Lizzie's contact, Matt, had not come to Scotland alone: he had brought two university friends, doctors, who treated us without asking questions and took Iris away, telling us she'd be safe.

Now Matt is hunched in front of the laptop, his face pale, twisting his itchy-looking moustache as he sees Christopher tell Ben that they're brothers.

I think about the clones back in the office. How many of *them* is Ben related to? I meet Ben's eyes. He looks as if he's been slapped across the face, his eyes are wide and shocked. I look at the ring on his finger. "If you're related to Gold..."

"Don't think about it, Grady. Not yet." Lizzie

grips my hand.

I start to smile. "When Gold dies…"

"Don't!" Lizzie repeats.

I look at Ben. "I'm just saying, it looks like he has a lot of kids out there. Psycho-kids. And if they find out that they're in a position to inherit… I don't think his little videos will stop them all."

With a jolt, Lizzie sits up. "A *lot* of kids?"

"Yes."

"Grady, the doctors who took Iris away…"

"What about them?"

"One of them … she looked a lot like Iris … don't you think?"

THE CON

Conspiracies You Can Believe   Written and edited by Grady Jackson

Gold's Secret Psychopaths

In the last issue, I wrote about Stowerling Keep and the terrifying secrets that lie in the ancient Gold family castle. Now I'm writing about the disappearance of the infamous Marcus Gold.

Gold vanished before he made it to court. With his assets frozen, the FBI demanding to speak to him and Interpol on the lookout, did he make it to a non-extradition country? Is he now sitting on a beach, or hiding in a consulate, awaiting transportation?

There are names that are forever linked to his now, and one of those is crime-lord Ian King, a man known for years by Scotland Yard, who have never been able to touch him.

My sources tell me that that he hasn't been seen since the week before the court case either. Then there're the claims of his children. Dozens have come forward, demanding DNA tests, wanting to be recognized by the courts.

His 'legitimate' offspring, Helen and Victoria Gold, have said that they will fight these newcomers, and that the family fortune will not be diluted among them.

To date, Christopher and Iris Gold remain missing, presumed dead. Would either of them have turned up for the court case? Now we may never know.

Last week I painted a picture of a man who desired to dominate the world, who wanted to place his offspring in positions of power across the globe. Did he imagine himself as King of the World? A hidden power, guiding the business and political landscape?

Now this is falling apart and, thanks to documentary evidence provided to lawyers by Mrs Carrie Harper, a new picture builds: of secret fertility clinics, unregulated research conducted in underground facilities, classified bases where young people, often his own sons and daughters, were tortured and killed in sick tests of their abilities and proclivities.

Which raises one final question... Is it truly possible to breed psychopaths? Can they be created through a baptism of fire? Is it nature or nurture that removes the conscience and creates utter ruthlessness?

And finally, how many of Gold's psychopaths remain at large; hidden in the world, perhaps not even knowing who they are? A new generation too young to take part in his sick games, an older generation too clever to come forward and show themselves.

How many did he create?

Acknowledgements

I would love to take this opportunity to thank everyone who contributed to making this book a reality: starting with Kate Williams and the rest of the wonderful team who run the Wirral Book Awards (and who honoured *Savage Island* and inspired *Cruel Castle*) and moving on to my tireless agent Catherine Pellegrino, my excellent editors Ruth Bennett and Mattie Whitehead, the rest of the team at Stripes and my wonderful husband and children (I love you, Andy, Maisie and Riley).

I would also really love to ask something of you, wonderful reader. I wrote this novel for you and if you read and enjoyed it, I've achieved what I set out to do. If you'd like to do something for me in return (and I hope you don't mind me asking), would you tell others to read it? Either spread the word when you're chatting with your friends, or leave a quick review (on Amazon or Goodreads, or even Twitter or Instagram)? It will make all the difference to me, as your review will help others find my book. Even if they're short and sweet, writers love to read your reviews, and we really appreciate hearing from our readers, it makes us feel as if we're making an impact.

Don't hold back. Write that review. Get in touch. Tell me what you thought. Tell me who you loved, who you hated, what parts made you shout, or cry, cringe or laugh. Tell me what you're writing, what you want to be. You can find me on Twitter (@BryonyPearce) or on Instagram (bryonypearce).

Like Grady's mum, I believe that strangers are mostly friends we haven't met yet. So, don't be a stranger!

About the Author

Bryony Pearce has always loved to write. She now has nine published young adult novels, *Angel's Fury* (2011, winner of both the Leeds Book Award and Cheshire Schools Book Award), *The Weight of Souls* (2013, UK and US), *Phoenix Rising* (2014, winner of the Wirral Grammar Schools best science fiction award), *Phoenix Burning* (2016, UK and US), *Wavefunction* (2016), *Windrunner's Daughter* (2016 and 2019 UK and US), *Savage Island* (2018, winner of Wirral Book Award, published in the UK, Turkey, Poland and Russia and translated into Arabic), *Raising Hell* (2021) and *Cruel Castle* (2021).

She also writes thrillers for adults. Her debut *The Girl on the Platform* came out in 2021, and her second is due out in 2022.

Bryony also writes short science fiction stories for adults, which have appeared in a number of anthologies.

Bryony can usually be found reading, writing, ferrying children from place to place and avoiding housework where possible. For more information about Bryony or her work do visit her website www.bryonypearce.co.uk or follow her on Instagram or Twitter @BryonyPearce.

Hunt or be hunted

SAVAGE ISLAND

BRYONY PEARCE

Find out how it all began…

Are you the best?
Are you driven to succeed?

A one million pound prize. Each. That's enough to
get five friends entering a geocaching competition.
But stranded on a remote island off the Scottish coast,
they soon realize this is no ordinary challenge.

The other teams are determined to win too.
Even if it means getting rid of the opposition.
Permanently.